I Am Barbarella

.

I Am Barbarella

Stories

Beth Gilstrap

Twelve Winters Press

Sherman, Illinois

Published by Twelve Winters Press.

P. O. Box 414 • Sherman, Illinois 62684-0414 • twelvewinters.com

I Am Barbarella was first published by Twelve Winters Press in 2015.

Cover and interior page design by TWP Design.

Cover image courtesy Jordyn Steiner. Used by permission. All rights reserved.

ISBN
978-0-9895151-8-4

Printed in the United States of America

Acknowledgments

Thank you to the literary magazines who published earlier versions of the following stories: "I Am Barbarella" first appeared in *Blue Fifth Review*'s Blue Five Notebook Series. "Yard Show" appeared in *the minnesota review.* "Machine" appeared in *Superstition Review.* "Juveniles Lack Green" originally appeared in *Quiddity.* "Some Girl" appeared in *Fwriction.* "Paper Fans" was published in *Columbia College Literary Review.* "Buddy and Lurch" and "Rosemarie Cuts the World" appeared in *Kudzu House Quarterly.* "Getting by with Sound" appeared in *Ambit Magazine.* "Quiet" appeared in *Stone Highway Review.* "After the Fire Is Gone" originally appeared in *Noctua Review*, and "Spaghettification" appeared in *Luna Luna Magazine.* Thank you to Ted Morrissey for your unwavering support and all you do for independent literature. Above all, I offer a heartfelt thank you to Ben. You are the love of my life. This book would never have happened without you to pick up the shattered mess of me time and time again. Thank you for believing in me even when I didn't. And thank you to the rest of my family and friends for instilling a deep love of creativity and radical empathy. I love you all. I would also like to thank the teachers who encouraged and inspired me including: Mrs. Moore, The Hastys, Mrs. Wicker, Ms. Brooks, Mrs. Helms, Aimee Parkison, Diane Goodman (who read and guided me through countless versions of this book), Sherrie Flick, Melanie Fox, Robert Yune, and Matt Hart. I would also like to thank Pamm Collebrusco, Adam Nicholson and Georgia Bellas for their editorial work throughout the process of bringing this book to print.

Contents

Visit the author's website, bethgilstrap.com, for a suggested playlist to accompany *I Am Barbarella*.

For Ben

I Am Barbarella

I am not meant to be alone
and without you who understands.

Carson McCullers
The Heart Is a Lonely Hunter

I Am Barbarella

The hair show is Russell's idea, not mine. He says, "Honey, that head is thick, shines like some auburn python. I could wrap up in it."

Russell and I spend most nights on the stoop of our duplex, smoking bowls and caressing the stray cats we feed. He pushes a paper bag my way. He's trying to pretty some backbone into me.

Upstairs, I have a good buzz when I pull my costume out. Randy's eyes gray, look pinched. "Should you be dressing like that, being a married woman and all?"

"Fuck, Randy, when will I ever get a chance to walk across a bar in vinyl boots and bloomers again?" I ask, putting my arms out and swinging my hips as I walk on my toes.

"I'm sure you could pole dance any time," he says. "You might even make some money looking like Elly May trash."

"Does that make you Jed Clampett?"

He sits on the corner of our rumpled bed and unlaces his combat boots. I cross my arms in front of the mirror. I am a projectile tiara. Wonder Woman's indestructible bracelets. I am Barbarella. I am Bettie Page. I am flat-chested, but my long legs make up for it. And the hair. It swings now, past my shoulder blades, tickling the backs of my arms. I build my armor with what I can. "You aren't the girl I used to know," he says.

We used to live off vending machine crackers. He favored Toast Chee and ate them stacked one on top of the other. I was the type to lick the filling off my Captain's Wafers first.

Before I quit school, I fumbled in the dark with a can opener, popping tops off film canisters, winding thin sheets of film around reels. With my fingernails, I'd separate the film from itself. I loved the sound of its wrinkle. If I stayed late, Randy would come talk to me through the door.

He rubs his temples.

"Didn't someone call the past a foreign country?" I ask.

When he walks out, his laces tap the hardwood. I stretch my arms out so wide my shoulders feel like they'll pull apart. It's as though I'm standing just beyond a storm of paper. I feel the fluttering but can't grab anything tangible.

At the salon, I get turned on when Russell teases my hair out and backcombs it into two little pigtails, curling at the bottoms like scorpions. My hair looks a little like an ass in the back with such a severe part down the middle, but the other stylists hover, congratulating Russell. He pulls a bottle of whiskey from his cabinet. Spacewomen and leather men toast with shots in paper cups as I unsnap my smock. We all pose in the shop before we pile in the van. Mr. Full-Sleeve-Tattoos stands next to me in his wife beater and silver pants, stares down at my red bloomers. I don't hide. I straddle a salon stool like it's a horse, throw my arm in the air. Cameras click.

A hulking bald man leads us all to the bar. A girl in a white wig falls. She pulls her skirt up to her shoulders, cackles. I'm last. A finale of skin and hairspray.

Now I'm one heel in front of the other, moving from the bar to the catwalk to queasy house music. I kick up one heel. Burn in my belly and my breasts. Feel eyes. I don't see Randy, but I worry he's seeing what I'm feeling.

When it's over, I stay in the clothes even as others change. I go out for a smoke. Russell hands me a shot of something caramel and sweet, says, "You did great, gal." He kisses my forehead. "Thanks for being my dolly."

"Anytime," I say, blowing liquor breath. I know I have to bury Barbarella.

Randy walks up, throws a cigarette down. A bouncing stub. I better get out of these clothes. Heat radiates to my face. His eyes. The eyes of the man I married—cast down. As I turn, I hear a drunk say, "That Elly May slut can wrestle me any day."

When I return, Randy is gone. I catch a ride from Russell.

"Fuck 'im," he says. "You're beautiful."

I lean my cheek on the passenger window. During the intro to a Led Zeppelin song, I can feel Randy's hand in my hair.

"Home?" Russell asks.

"Home," I say.

YARD SHOW

It ain't garbage if you turn it into something. Something slow-dipped and pulled apart. Put back together again upside down. Round side out. Glib. Free. A vulture made of wire hangers. Fabric ripped, draped, coated in splash zone compound. Shingle seals barking up at spraying feathers.

I got a scrap heap under a tarp up in the back yard. Sunday, that's my girl's name, says it's all junk. I need to get shit of it if I want her to move in with me. I can't picture her up in here, though. She's too pretty. Got long nails and a sweep of collarbone that gets me off task. I'm just fine with her uptown at her tidy little woman's place with fresh sheets and curtains and all.

My house is about as bad as my yard. I keep buckets of empty spray paint cans in the kitchen. Paint done gone to its place in the spotlight on other yard shows. One bucket colored a great big rooster up on Dunlop Street. That one was commissioned. Not really a yard show if it's city-funded, I guess. Still, my big cock gonna last a long time, I like to say. I plan on taking a mallet to those cans, smashing them flat. I got paper bags of old beer cans. They make my house smell sour, but one day they'll be tall black-eyed Susans jutting out from an old tire swing. I'll run the chains bolted to the tire with ribbon, maybe nylons. Colored L'eggs nylons—that kind that comes in a plastic egg at the drugstore for fifty cents.

I got an old carpet remnant rolled up in the corner. It could have some cat pee on it, but I say that just adds to it. Going to be a piece for all the senses and Lord knows a sense of smell is a right powerful thing. An eagle will hang from barbed wire. Maybe some old bamboo fishing poles, tie some ripped scarves to the top so they can catch the wind, and decorate my yard with whipping fabric, wind-dancing blues and muddy purples. They can hang limp during rain showers, dry hard in the sun. Grow green spots of mold. Start to disintegrate.

Those high-art folk like to talk about decay these days. Painting in blood. Horseshit, I say. We been doing this down South ages. Yard show part land, part weather, part human, part not. It jump together up in you and you can't shake it. There's codes in things, maybe you don't know. That sofa on the side of the road got story, too.

My show out front of my own place got a robot made of scrap metal and tools my granddaddy give me before he died. I put his hammer where a heart should be. I like the way the blue paint's worn almost completely away and it's slick down in the spots where he held it. He's been gone near to thirty years, but I got an object his hand wore down to smooth.

I'm carrying buckets of paint cans to the back when Sunday yells from the other side of the fence. "All this stuff. How can you stand it? You're gonna get rats."

She put one arm on top of the other, covering the lion at the top of the gate. In her red shorts, Sunday's skin pressed through the chain-link. All that flesh and metal made me think of meat grinders. And there it was, that slope from neck to shoulder. I want my mouth on it when I die. If there's a God, an honest to true higher power looking out for me, he'll make that happen.

"I ain't seen a durn rat yet. If I do, I'll just trap it, skin it, dry its bones and use them in a piece."

"That's disgusting," she said, opening the squeaky gate. She put her hands in her back pockets, walked right up to me, planted one on my cheek. "But I love you anyway."

"You, too," I said, putting the buckets down and throwing one leg over the bench I'd carved from a walnut tree that fell in a storm some years back. I'd cut the log down in the thick branch of its middle where the grain was like tight waves, almost curls. She sat down too, facing forward, stretching her long legs. Sunday slipped off her shoes and dug at the dirt and grass with her big toes. She had a bunion on one but that didn't bother me. A working woman usually does. "Feel like swinging a mallet?" I asked.

"Can I pretend it's my boy's head when I bring it down instead of some old paint can?"

"Sure enough. What he do now?" I asked, pulling the mallet from my tool belt, and setting a lid and can on the bench between us.

She stood, brought the mallet up over her head and swung hard, gritting her teeth while she done it. The lid goes flying, lands over by the fence.

"He says he'd rather live with his daddy."

I push the can over a bit. "It's your ex-husband," I say. "Not the boy. Son of a bitch's putting ideas in his head."

She pulls the mallet back again, stares down at that can like it done everything wrong in this world. In her swing, she yells, "Motherfucker!" and it crumples like you wouldn't believe. Sunday knows. She's part of this yard show.

MACHINE

Charlotte, North Carolina, 1988

Tight in her joints, Sue worked her machine, all the while yammering to Janine what life was like in mill housing. With a husband who couldn't read much, sewing came in handy. He made what money he could manning a school bus and mowing yards around the neighborhood. Either way, he came home drenched and stinking like onion.

"We only had the one room. Saturday was bath day and since I was the youngest the water was cold gray slop by the time I got in." Sue pumped the pedal, worked the hand dial, and followed the pattern lines. Stopping, she rubbed the fleshy bit of her palm, working her way up her thumb. "Can you believe that? I'd always be mad at my brothers and sisters for taking so long. They'd set the tub up in front of the fireplace but it didn't do much good. Half of you was always cold."

Janine tried to listen at first, but she got lost in Grandma Sue's button collection. Matching them, making designs out of them. Smiley faces. Rainbows. Trees. Houses.

"That one looks like our house. One door on the front. One window on each side," Sue said.

"One of the shutters is falling down on the front of mine and Daddy's house."

"Why hasn't your father fixed it?" Sue asked as the machine's pulse stopped. She dropped a pillow on the floor and seated herself next to Janine. As they dug through buttons together, Sue hoped she could get back up without falling on her face. Rolling a gilt button over her fingers like a quarter, she got Janine's attention.

"He says because Mom left and he can't do everything. Says that to himself a lot. I hear him talking when nobody's around."

Janine fiddled with a few buttons of different sizes, but each one slipped from between her fingers. Wiping the house away, she scooped up a handful of buttons and dropped them back in the tin. Sue ripped a piece of yellow paper from her notepad and scooped some. With the last few, Janine pushed her pointer finger into them until they stuck. As she flicked them, the clacks made rhythm.

"Well, try to go easy on your father. He's had a hard time of it. You behave like the little lady you are and I'll get you a makeup kit for your twelfth birthday."

"Dad says I can't wear makeup yet," she said, standing.

"Well, it'll be our secret. Just make sure you wash it off before he sees it." Sue reached her hand up to Janine. "Help me up." Holding onto her granddaughter with one hand and the bedpost with another, she struggled to keep her balance. "Hold that tiger."

Janine laughed. "What the heck's that mean? Who's got a tiger?" As Sue sat on the edge of the bed, Janine put the button tin on the vanity and smoothed her hair.

"It's just something my father used to say," she said, tapping her tingling foot on the floor. "He'd say it whenever he slammed on brakes in the car. Don't say heck, it's barely a step up from hell. There, that's got it. Now, let's go get something to eat. I've got country ham and I can throw some Pillsbury biscuits in the oven. I might even have some cheddar left. Does a ham and cheese sound good to you?"

"Sounds awesome." Janine stood in front of the vanity. "Do you think I look like my mother?"

"Well, I don't know what she looked like when she was young, but you do seem to have her coloring, her hair. We could ask Rachel to cut it short if it bothers you."

"I don't really care," she said, moving closer to the mirror.

In the kitchen, Sue pulled the ham out of orange Tupperware. When she felt the cold salt grit between her fingers, her stomach growled. Somehow, she was back to pulling fat off meat. Popping a bit in her mouth, she sucked it until it lost flavor. She couldn't understand why kids wouldn't eat the best part. Leaving fat scraps in a paper towel, she got the last nub of cheddar from the dairy drawer and sliced it on the counter.

"What do you want to drink?" Sue asked as she got down two wine glasses.

"Do you have any Sprite? I'm not supposed to drink caffeine."

Janine sat at the kitchen table, tapping her fingers against the metal edge. It was so cramped in the kitchen that Sue had pushed the table against the wall where you couldn't even get to one chair. She figured only she and Janine and Janine's granddad, William, ever used that table. When company came, they spread out in the dining room.

"I think so. Go check in the closet in the little room."

Sue had helped as much as she could with Janine since her drunk of a daughter-in-law left her son. She and William had helped Hardy look for Loretta, even talked to the police. Sue told him from the beginning Loretta had abandoned them, that Hardy needed to face facts.

Another man and a heap of booze is what happened to her. Sue had never said another word about the woman; she just pretended she didn't exist, that somehow Hardy had hatched his little darling on his own. This was hard to do considering she looked just like her absent Mama. But Sue liked being there for Janine. When Hardy was a boy, she spent most of her waking hours working at the mill.

Hardy and Janine came over for supper on Sundays and they kept Janine whenever Hardy needed time to himself. Sue had encouraged him to start dating again for several years now, but if he did he never told her about it. She even tried to fix him up with Rachel's girl but no one championed that idea except her so it fizzled before it even had a chance to get going.

Janine came in with a two-liter of Sprite. "Found it."

"Good, now get some ice and I'll pour it for us."

When Sue poured the soda, she blew on it so it wouldn't fizz over. "What do you want to do this afternoon?"

"Can Maddie come over? We could ride our bikes up to the park."

"You two can't go a minute without one another, can you?"

Janine nibbled at her biscuit.

"Something wrong with the ham?" Sue asked.

"No, Grandma, it's good."

"Well go on and call her, then." Sue said before taking a big bite of her own biscuit. "Mmm. I don't know how you can turn your nose up at this."

"I'm not turning my nose up." Janine took polite bites until she thought she'd eaten enough to satisfy her grandmother. She propped her elbows on the table. Sue noticed a beetle-shaped scab on her right arm.

"Lord, child. What have you done to yourself now?"

Janine looked down at the scab and poked at it with her first and middle fingers. "It's getting better. At least it's hard now. Itch-es though," she said as she scratched the pink skin around the edges.

"But how did it happen? That's going to leave a scar if you're not careful. You better start putting some vitamin E on it when the scab falls off and don't pick at it."

"I fell off the shed," Janine said. Her eyes widened and she broke into a fat grin.

Sue sighed, pushing back her empty plate. "What am I going to do with you, girl? What were you doing on the shed? Where was your father?"

"I climb up there sometimes when I need to think about stuff. There's a pine tree next to it, and I can put my back against the wall and my feet on the tree and sort of push myself up. I get up on top and sit with one leg on each side of the, the . . ."

"The pitch?"

"Yeah," she said, dropping half a biscuit into the trash.

"Just put that other one on the counter. I'm sure your grand-daddy will eat it when he gets home." Janine wiped her hands on the back of her jeans. "Well," Sue said. "How'd you fall?"

"I was about to get down and I stood up and walked to the front. I usually just jump down onto the ramp from there, but I got dizzy. I just kind of fell over. My arm hit the ramp, but I landed in the grass. I didn't even realize I was bleeding at first. It turned white, then the blood came."

"It's a wonder you didn't break your neck. Was that your only injury?"

"I've got a couple bruises, one big one here," she said, rubbing her right hip.

"So, where was your father?"

"Asleep in front of the TV. He came and helped me up. He said I screamed when I fell but I don't think I did, at least I don't remember it. He washed the dirt out of my elbow with the kitchen sink sprayer then poured alcohol on it and put on a Band-Aid."

"You make me think you need eyes on you all the time. You better not go up there anymore. What did your dad say?"

"Not to climb up there anymore."

"Good," Sue said. "What did you have to think about up on the shed?" She stood and walked over behind Janine and rubbed her shoulders. Janine had several different tan lines. One from her T-shirts and another from her striped bathing suit she wore when they went to the YMCA. She was a good swimmer. Always had been. Her mother had taken her for lessons when she was two years old. Her mother liked to lounge around the pool, sneak liquor in her purse, and pour it into plastic red cups and bake herself like pottery while Janine swooshed her way around the pool all day. They'd drop by sometimes, and Sue would comb the knots out of Janine's hair while Loretta napped on the couch. She'd spray leave-in conditioner in her hair and work at it from the bottom up.

"You want me to comb your hair for you? Do a French braid maybe?" Sue asked, tickling Janine's neck.

"Nah, I'm good," she said. "Guess I'll call Maddie now."

"All right," Sue said, disappointed and feeling nostalgic for when Janine was younger. She knew she'd start drifting further and further away in the coming years, just like her father had done. Just like all teenagers. She'd start getting interested in boys, if she wasn't already. Sue had had her first kiss when she was thirteen. On one of those carnival rides that twirls cages upside down. She and a boy named Bobby had met at the Memorial Day parade downtown and then run into each other again. Their friends had teased them and coaxed them into riding rides together. They held hands walking around and Bobby had leaned forward in the cage to press his lips to her, but the cage spun then and their faces had mostly landed on each other. She and her friends had agreed that it counted. Bobby wrote her a letter a few weeks later. He lived down East, at the coast, near Hatteras. He wrote how he wished he could move to Charlotte, saying how once the tourists left, the beach was boring. In fall, he'd look for sea turtle nests and one time, he said, he'd been lucky enough to see some hatchlings headed to the water. He'd walked down that night with a flashlight in each pocket and his parents' Polaroid.

Janine didn't talk about boys, though. Sue didn't blame her. She didn't figure a girl wanted to share secrets with her grandma.

Janine picked the phone up and carried it off to the closet, the cord curling around the corner and under the door.

When Sue passed by, she put her ear to the door for a moment.

"Grandma says it's cool if you come over. Do you want to come here and then you can sleep over? Dad will pick us up tonight. Maybe we can get him to take us to the movies."

"I'll take you to the movies," Sue said, cracking the door.

Janine was sitting Indian-style on the floor, the bottoms of her feet dusted brown. Sue thought it was about time she cleaned the floors again. "You know, Grandma, you really shouldn't be eavesdropping."

"I wasn't. Just passing through on the way to the bathroom."

"Whatever," Janine said, wrapping the cord around her wrist until her hand began to turn purple.

"Stop that. Your hand will fall off if you don't watch it."

"Yeah right. If you don't mind," she said, looking up.

"We'll see," Sue said.

Sue spent the afternoon working on a new pair of coveralls for William. She wanted to make some for Hardy, too, but he'd told her to stop making clothes for him a long time ago. It wasn't worth the trouble when he could get what he needed from Wal-Mart cheap. Sue had always wanted another child but for some reason or another never conceived again. She figured something was wrong with her but had never had the courage to find out for sure. Women in her family were funny about going to that kind of doctor. No one ever talked about how babies came to be. She planned to have a frank and detailed discussion with Janine if Hardy would let her. She figured he'd be too squeamish to tell her about her monthlies anyway.

Sue finished the hem by hand before William got home and before Hardy came to pick up the girls. She could have relaxed and watched some TV, but she got the ironing board out and worked on getting the wrinkles out of the new outfit she'd created for her husband. Idle time made her stomach hurt.

She sprayed starch down one leg. The iron sizzled on the denim and the fabric smoothed out easily. The house settled in around her as it got dark out. The crickets picked up their volume. She'd stood so long in the mill days that now it felt like bone on bone in her hips when she sat down for long stretches. She had worked the show table for nearly thirty years by the time she retired. Throwing big bolts of fabric over her shoulder earned her the men's respect and more than one glance. These days, her flesh swung from her bones.

She heard the garage door open. William walked in with sweat stains down to his waist. She lifted the coveralls up for his approval. "What do you think of these? Can you use them?"

"Sure enough," he said. "These might walk off on their own."

"You hungry?"

"I could eat." He walked over to the sink, splashed some water in his face, and reached for the towel she had Janine's leftover biscuit in.

"Use paper towels," she fussed. "There's a biscuit in the towel for you."

"Oh," he said. "Ham?" He leaned against the counter, left the wet paper towel on the edge of the sink. "Maddie here too? Where are those ragamuffins?"

"Out riding bikes. Maybe at the park. Probably flirting with boys."

"I'm so glad we didn't have a girl. Seems like more trouble."

"You should see the raspberry on her elbow," she said, folding up the ironing board. William ate his biscuit with one hand under his mouth. The last time they'd been intimate he'd had to stop. She hoped that wouldn't be the last time they'd try. Even after all these years and going through menopause, she still craved him. She'd lie awake at night thinking about it. Sometimes, she'd get up and sew something or clean. She couldn't stand to sit up in bed with the little book light he'd given her. Romance novels just added to the problem anyway.

"Do I need to put some iodine on it?"

"No, it's about healed now. Your son was asleep in his glider rather than watching her. She fell off the shed."

"Well, Jesus."

"Don't say Jesus like that," she said. "Why don't you go get cleaned up before Hardy gets here? If he gets here before you get out, I'll make him stay. Lord knows when those girls will pull up. I told them to be home by the time the streetlights came on but here it is and you see they haven't showed yet."

"I reckon I will. Can I get a hug and kiss?" he asked, walking toward her.

"I don't think so, mister. Not until you take a shower."

When William shrugged his shoulders and went upstairs, Sue finally sat down in the den. The heating pad would feel good to her right now, but she stayed put. Opening the bottle of Tylenol on the end table, she shook three pills into her palm. Since she swallowed without water, they sat in her esophagus like pebbles.

Somewhere below the pain, she remembered what it felt like to be her granddaughter's age. Since she went to work at sixteen, it was that time before adolescence when she felt the strongest. Running in the fields behind their house, she'd push herself hard until she felt the ground move up from her soles to her knees and through her hips. Until bath day, she always looked a little greasy from the exercise.

Upstairs, the pipes rumbled as William started the water. Her first real shower had been on their honeymoon. They'd stayed in a motel on the way to Myrtle Beach. They couldn't wait the four hours it would take to drive to the beach. William had unbuttoned the thirty-two buttons she'd put down the back of the dress she'd sewn. She'd told him to be careful, she wasn't sure how good her work was yet. His fingers worked quicker than she'd expected and instead of carrying her to the bed, he'd taken her standing up, against the door.

Afterwards, in the shower, she had washed her wedding day makeup away with a tinge of regret. Now what? She had wondered, letting the heat work into her muscles.

When the front door opened, she heard heavy steps and the squeals of young girls.

"Ma?" Hardy yelled, "Where you at? I'm here for the girls. Found them up the street."

She met them in the kitchen. "Here I am. I was just sitting down for a minute. Can I fix you something to eat before you go?"

The girls kissed her on the cheek and walked back out as quickly as they'd entered. "Bye, Grandma Sue!" they both said, letting the screen door slam.

Sue rubbed her eyes with her thumbs.

"They give you any trouble?" Hardy asked, pulling out a chair at the kitchen table.

"No trouble, but I saw where she fell."

"I know, I know. I should've been watching her. She knows she's not to get back up on that shed."

"Think she'll listen?"

"Doubt it," he said. "Where's Dad?"

"Upstairs in the shower. Hungry?"

"Nah. I should really get going. I told the girls I'd take them for pizza and drop them off at the movies."

"Wait for your father. He wanted to say hello."

"Tell him hi for me, and I'll see him next weekend."

"Well, don't hurry," she said, putting her hand on his cheek.

"I'm not trying to, but these girls, you know how it is."

"I certainly do," she said. "Hey, listen, maybe next time you head to the beach we can tag along."

"Sure, Ma," he said, reaching for the door. "Sounds like a plan."

As she turned the lamp off in the living room, the headlights moved across the wall and disappeared. In the dark, she cracked her knuckles and finally sat down.

Juveniles Lack Green

Moss and algae on creek rocks make me keep a close watch on my feet. It'd be my luck to roll an ankle out here on my own. No cell service. I got a whistle, that's about it. Maybe the Saint Bernards I saw down the mountain would come barreling up, all slobbery if they heard it, but they seemed cooped up and ornery in their pen.

Water's colder here than it is back home this time of year. I could stick my bare feet in, plant my butt on a rock, and just sit until a good sweat formed on my back. Not here. Here I'm layered up like Angie's yellow cakes. A fleece and two jackets ain't quite enough.

I wished I'd packed something sweet. Fourteen days since my last brownie or anything. It would help if I knew how to cook too. All this Chef Boyardee I'm heating on the hotplate ain't doing much for me. Rumbling insides aren't great when you're trying to be quiet and find some critters.

On the log, a male Steller's jay cocks his head. I like the way he looks like a punk rocker. Lots of bright blue and jet-black and that tuft sticking straight up. His mate is up a ways on that moss-covered lichen-dripping whatever it is. They look like they're onto me.

He looks as if he'd say, "Junebug, get a look at this idiot in the creek."

And the darker blue female would answer, "Yeah Papa, I swooped in yesterday to get a closer look. I think he's wearing Polo."

I'm kidding myself, really. I thought after Angie left this would be a good way to put some cushion between the garbage of us. She's still mad as hell and I can't blame her. That woman down in Atlanta was close to seven years ago. People say I was stupid to tell her, but she hadn't touched me in over a year anyway, so I figured I might as well get it out. Maybe it'd help cut down on my migraines. But why I thought it'd be a good idea to cross the country in my faded Dodge pickup and hole up in a log cabin in Oregon is beyond me.

I should have started growing my beard in the day I threw my duffel in the truck. Me and Johnny Cash cutting across old roads through sick storms and worse heat, through everyday towns and nowhere towns and some kind of David Lynch towns you wouldn't dare stop in for fear of characters talking backwards in red rooms and dead, blonde teenagers.

It feels like Wednesday, but I can't be sure. There's a real in-the-middle-of-things air about the place. The sun's going down. Between the mountains, it gets dim faster. I miss the low country sunsets, the smell of Angie's Frogmore stew boiling, the spicy sausage, crab, and corn mixing like some kind of redneck aphrodisiac. Here, it smells sweet and clear and clean. I wish I could take a bit of paper and charcoal and do a rubbing on my brain to get it to soak in.

When I stand, my butt's gone numb. So much for bird watching. All I saw was another brick-colored salamander and the same pair of jays. It was only after I got bored of playing solitaire and blackjack that I picked up *Birds of the Willamette Valley*. It set there next to the record player for at least a week before I even noticed it. I'd played *Abbey Road* so much I started to hate it, but most everything else the owner had left in the place was classical or opera or show tunes. Makes me wish I'd thrown a box of records or CDs in the truck, too, but I can always go find a record shop if I get desperate.

The creek sounds better than *Abbey Road*, and that's good enough for now. I flipped through the book, folding down the edges of the birds I thought I'd seen. Robins. Chickadees. Crows. I even think I saw a little bushtit, and boy did that sucker tell me to get the hell on my way. Cute little guy. Can't say that I blame him. But when I saw the violet-green swallow's photo, that's when I got serious. I went looking and listening. Only two weeks here and I sit in creek beds, straining my ears for a song that's supposed to sound like *tsip tseet tsip*. Can't say I know exactly what that will sound like when I hear it, though. I wonder if the T is silent, but it's got to be more about the rhythm. I just want to see the green on that bird. Book says the male's back is *glossy, iridescent-purple-green* with white reaching above its eye.

The taste of tomato on my ravioli is shallow, feels like wet cardboard in my mouth. Thumbing through the bird book again, I figure I might as well venture out at dawn. Seems like everyone's active then. Rereading the description of the female, I wonder how, in nature, females are always more subdued. My experience with women is opposite, but maybe it's society telling women they have to shine up for us, get skinny, have some kind of never-ending youth where they never show any seasoning or character. Angie looked better to me once she quit dying her hair black. She had this great chestnut auburn thing happening, and the sun bleached it even lighter in the summer, especially when she lay on the beach on her days off, encouraging her skin to spot and darken.

The juveniles lack green. In the morning, I'll try again.

My walking stick sinks in spongy ground. The forest drips, and I can hear Angie's voice drifting from the kitchen through the hall and into the living room where I watch the Clemson game. I can't say she had a good voice, but it always made me want to grab her, even when she was cooking, which I'd learned a long time ago was not cool. If I could change what happened with Whatshername, I would. All I even remember of that night at this point is a motel room that smelled like Fritos and the crunch of hairspray in her hair. Angie and I hadn't made love in four or five months and this bartender in a Mexican joint talked sweet to me. I drank just enough bottom-shelf tequila to lose good sense. Can't say I didn't do it. Can't say I didn't screw myself ten ways to Sunday, but I'd hoped since so much time had passed and I'd come clean, Angie might try to understand. When

I finally get still in the woods, I hear it, the courtship song male violet-green swallows sing in the minutes before dawn. It's about time my own green shows.

SOME GIRL

The van was all hot breath and man stink, so I closed my eyes, resting my head against the fogged window. This was what I wanted—to be squished next to Brandon and headed west where the country unfolds until its spine's exposed, flat and easy to leave, a good spot to mark for return, a pause. This land was always right where you left her. The sound of rubber on asphalt merged with an Iron Maiden song blaring from Steve's headphones. Turn the volume down on everything but her. Clenching my jaw, I tried my best to push age on my girl's face, to add six months to it, subtract baby teeth, but try as I might, she looked the same. She stayed a fresh seven-year-old in my head, with her wiggling incisor and flurry of birthday energy lifting her hair as she danced and drew and built a fort.

"Come see, Mom. Come see," she said.

"I see, baby." Only her legs visible under her tarp house. White ruffled socks in purple clogs. Mud splatters from yesterday's rain. When she was thinking, her right foot crossed behind the left, a little tic that gave her away.

This is what happens when you run.

Whole days showered in freezing rain, turned hard to touch, worse to navigate, but maybe, almost prettier behind that sheet of ice, but you can't get home, not for a long stretch, and it's preserved and out of reach in you. Bourbon or sun or open road don't fix it.

"Turn that shit down," I said. "You are killing me."

"What's that, doll?" Jay asked over his shoulder.

"Not you. Steve's music's loud as shit. Does he ever listen to anything aside from Maiden?"

"He thinks if he listens to it enough, he'll sound like Bruce

Dickinson."

"Christ, is that it?"

"Climb up here with me. They're passed out anyways."

As I angled my shoulder down, Brandon's head lolled to his chest. His hand slid off my thigh and landed palm up, showing the number some girl wrote on his palm. Last night, all I could do was smile at the little thing with her Sun-In orange hair and shove him in the van. Girl has no idea. She'll be little more than smudged marker on their hands before long. Where she's headed, these band guys will chew her to bone. She won't know spooling herself around these guys doesn't save you any more than walking into the eye of a hurricane, but sometimes you got to go on thinking you're some kind of buffalo.

On the next seat up, Rory curled into himself like an insect, his hair hanging over his eyes. "Where are we?" I asked, climbing over the cooler.

"On 412. Next town's Orienta. Passed Fairview a few miles back. Ever heard of it?"

"May have passed through here with Daddy as a kid. Fairview, I mean."

"When you were a kid, huh? Must've been about four years ago?"

"Is that flirting or are you just a moron?"

"Both, maybe," he said as he fished for a beer. "Running low." He wiped the wet can on his jeans.

"Guess I'll take the attention where I can get it. Brandon seems to hold all the stock in flirt, lately."

"You ain't used to that by now? You've been with us a while."

"Some nights I'm okay with it. Some nights not so much. Don't make any sense, I know, but hell. I'm not sure how much sense is in this van."

"This shit ain't easy. Not sure we'll ever get to the point where we don't have to work like hell to sell records. I don't expect to fill superdomes like Steve does."

"You don't really seem like rock gods."

"Aren't you supposed to be our little cheerleader?"

"Right. You got me pegged. It's just, other than Brandon, you're a bit timid for heavy-duty spotlights."

"I guess."

"I mean it as a compliment. You're purer that way. Something about all this glam shit now jags my heart. These boys and what's that chick group?"

"Vixen."

"Right. So many of these bands took a wrong turn and just said to hell with it. A devil baby made from disco's day-old crotch and the stinking armpit of rock. Give me Patty Smyth and Scandal over Vixen any day."

"Must be all the coke."

"Anyway, I'm glad I hang with guys who care more about music than image and women. There's still pieces of the blues in your songs. Poetry even."

"It's nice someone notices. I'm waiting, though. Waiting for Brandon to take it another direction," he said.

We both knew what was coming.

"God, look. You ever see mountains shine like that?"

At the horizon, the land rose sharp into buttes. Jay and I kept our eyes forward on the formations, gathering light and dark and reflecting so much more than the physics of musicians careening in the guts of a blue conversion van. I could tell it'd be a good bit colder when we got out, but I didn't dig for another layer, just buttoned my jacket and unrolled the bowls I'd formed at my elbows.

"Looks like a good spot for a walk," Jay said, leaning over.

"It's thick in here anyway," I said, with my boots propped on the dash. "And my legs are getting twitchy."

"I only got about twenty minutes till I piss myself anyway. Should be there by then, I'd think."

I flipped the tape to side B of Meddle. In the twenty minutes it took us to get there, we zoned in and out. Gliding into piano tinks, we tiptoed on puddles. Razed by guitar, shattered in bird screams. Into the swell of momentum and pulled back down again, just so. Gotta hand it to Floyd. In all my life, I never expressed anything so true. Just once, just once, I'd like to stand up and say my piece and have someone respond. You can find so much on B-sides.

As we pulled up to the sign, Jay read, "Gloss Mountains. Hours: Dawn–Dusk."

"We got time. Sun's not down yet."

"No, but we won't make it to the top before it goes down," he said.

"See what I mean? What a poor excuse for a musician. Nothing but a rule follower at your core."

When I poked him in the chest, he finally cut his eyes my direction. "Like hell," he said, putting the last two beers in his pockets.

"That's what I like to hear."

He ran ahead of me, as fast as he could until he shifted into silhouette. When he slowed to a walk, his strides became long and heavy. In his wake, I stretched to fit my feet in his prints. Putting my heels in his made me more of a little girl than I'd been since my sisters and I ran topless around the lake, too young to know or care about modesty. I wondered how one could feel ten and be my age, broad-thighed and drinking my weight in bourbon, holding onto a man I didn't really want because I could. I know my body was lanky once. The air changed pressure and temperature; I felt myself drifting as if made of helium and housed in purple latex, tied tight with a bow, loose.

It's mostly the road, now. Brandon has an apartment back in Raleigh, but hell if I'm staying there alone while they're off playing shows. Six months into this thing for real, still partners in crime, boozing nights and days, sleeping naked, sometimes alone, sometimes in a room full of people, I don't do mirrors much anymore. I've lost cheekbones. But I'm free. I'm free. These boys don't expect me to take care of them. I fell into their fold and I'll be tucked in deep until we reach our caustic end. God knows it'll be bitter. Anything but would be a shining miracle.

I saw Jay's legs before the rest of him. "You know, I love that you only ever wear black jeans."

"Well, I'm not wearing that acid washed shit," he said, wiping red dust off his knees."

"Like mine?"

"That's different. You're a woman."

"Oh, right." I pulled my hair up into a high ponytail. "I forgot."

"You up for it?"

"Yeah, why not? Though if I'd known there'd be hiking on this trip, I'd have brought tennis shoes."

"We could go up barefoot."

"We'd probably get better traction," I said, pointing at the slick bottom of my boots.

"We must be out of our gourds."

"No arguments there, brother."

When we threw our boots behind us, I shook off that inward way, that way that gets my back all knotted up and has me reaching for the bottle when there's still hours of sunlight left. Our feet got air and dirt. As we approached the bottom of the tallest peak, we smiled at each other. He ran until the grade became too steep. Neither of us could get enough momentum in tight pants.

"Maybe we should take our pants off," he said.

"Wouldn't that be a picture?"

"Come on, girl. You can do it."

"I'm coming, I'm coming." Looking down, he had a double chin. "But the pants are staying on." When I was close enough, he reached for me.

"Shame we aren't pants-less. How are the feet?"

"Dirty and cold."

"Like my ex."

"You are full of yourself today."

We continued on. He was first over every outcrop, pushing himself up with small grunts. Pebbles fell into my hair and on my shoulders and it wasn't long before my mouth tasted like iron and clay.

"You okay?" Jay asked at the base of the summit. "One more push."

"Not sure I have anything left."

"One more push, doll, then we're there. I got you."

"If you say so," I said feeling like my elbows would snap in two.

"Bravo. You made it."

With raised eyebrows, Jay crouched down, turned his hand up, and motioned wide. From the flat top, we could see oil rigs in the distance. A pair of buzzards looped in a slow figure eight. I wondered what kind of body lay out there on that red expanse, just out of my eyeline, drying out under the sun into those bleached desert bones people put on fireplaces. They disgusted me, sure, but something about them called for touch, to feel those natural cracks in skulls, how similar we are to porcelain on the inside. Once we lose our connective tissue, we can show softer to those that put their hands on us.

Jay was there, but I lost track of him.

Walking the perimeter, I soaked up arid dusk. I had loved a good man and I had left him and before I knew it, my leg slipped out from under me.

"You okay?"

"Still here."

"Not for lack of trying. Of all places to zone out. Can you stand?"

"Not sure. Something cracked in my ankle."

"Well, come on, let's try to get you up." He put his shoulder under my arm, anchored himself and stuck a finger in my belt loop. "You in or out, girl?"

"Count me out," I said leaning away.

"I'm not sure what to do here."

Patting the ground, I said, "Sit with me. We'll figure it out in a minute."

All my blood seemed to gather in my foot and multiply. I

pulled my leg out from under me with both hands. With our legs draped over the edge of the butte, his swinging like a kid's off the back of a truck, he asked me what no one else had the nerve to.

"Have you talked to your daughter yet?"

"No," I said. "I'm not ready."

"Fair enough, but . . ."

"I don't want to talk about it, Jay."

"It gets better."

"Does it?"

"Well, you get to the point where you don't think about them all the time."

"I don't think about her as much as you'd think."

"But she creeps in, doesn't she? She was on your mind when you fell. Some kind of self-punishment. Like those self-lashing priests."

"It's not like that at all."

"What then?"

"I was thinking about bones. What difference does it make? I'm not going back. Not for a long time."

"Can I ask you a question?"

"No."

He moved his leg so it touched mine. Pain seared its way from my toes to my waist.

"Why'd you leave? It can't just have been Brandon."

"Jesus." He leaned his head against mine. "How many ways can I say to leave it alone?"

"You just don't seem the type. Brandon goes for ones like last night."

"Thanks."

"It's just—you're substantial. His girls usually aren't. That's all."

"Did you know porcelain's actually pretty tough?"

"I've heard."

"What do you suppose the white is in the mountains? Looks like the same crystals hippies wear. Maybe we can align our chakras by default."

"My money's on gypsum. The stuff of plaster. You can build with it," Jay said.

"Substantial."

"Yes."

"The truth is, I don't even remember meeting Brandon. Had to be at one of your shows—me in all my substance and leather, latched onto him. If I try hard enough, I can envision you guys on stage, the light behind his hair, his hands on that guitar, but that could be recent shit I'm projecting on what I can't remember."

"When was the exact moment you decided?"

"There was this morning," I said, pressing my shin where it had started to swell.

"Wait," Jay said. "Let's try to head down. We won't have any light left before long. The guys are bound to be awake soon if they aren't already."

We repeated the earlier maneuver, shoulders and a barefoot man trying to get leverage enough to lift me. When I was finally up, we both looked out toward the birds. One had landed.

"Wonder what he's got?"

"Wonder if he'll share? A part of me wants my body lain out in the open when I die."

"Not me," he said, shifting his weight. "I want a funeral pyre. On a boat. A beautiful woman to shoot a flaming arrow at my carcass."

"Well, shit, Jay. You don't want much, do you?"

"Let's get back to the van."

We half slid down the trail, and by the time we got back, he'd scraped his hand. Rory and Brandon had climbed up on top of the van.

"What happened to you two?" Brandon asked.

"Just unprepared hiking. She needs a doctor."

"But we got that show in Amarillo," Rory said as he slid down the windshield to tap on the hood. Drummers always had their sticks and, without fail, tested damn near every surface. The only drummer I didn't want to smack was one on stage.

"That ain't till ten. Nothing but time, brother."

"I'll be okay. I can get some ice when we eat."

"Right. Let's get some food," Brandon said. "I'll drive. You're up front with me."

"I need to stretch this leg. I'll sit in the back with Steve."

"Shotgun," Rory said.

Miles and meals passed. There was always some girl and always would be. I never answered Jay's question—not even once I'd started sleeping with him, too. One night he stood next to me for the opening band. Quiet for a few songs, he finally said, his voice fighting the drum solo, "I should've let you tell me when I had the chance."

They played their shows. I walked through crowds, thin and thick, forgetting time and days; moments churned together. There were days I felt three-quarters into some other B-side, lost in its momentum, wondering when iron and clay would settle.

Paper Fans

Janine tosses her and Maddie's coats up in the corner like some black heap of animal carcass. Alone, her petite frame gets lost in the booth. Janine's eyes are caked in liquid liner, curling cat-like at the corners, punctuated at the ends with three dots. The burned out letters BBQ hanging on the opposite wall look their age. Janine's mind felt the same, like charred paint flakes on metal shells. This is the Diamond's second life, but it's been open in some fashion since the '50s. It smells like burnt tomato sauce, fryer grease, and cigarettes. Janine unbuttons her wallet before ordering, trying to decide whether the silver or blue Visa has more room on it. No one was buying much furniture these days. Her store was in trouble.

She orders fried pickles. Two junior blocks with chili. Pitcher of Pabst.

Maddie comes out of the bathroom flinging water from her hands. She looks the same now as she did when they were seven, the same full mouth, the same bony knees, only now she dyed her hair black and collected tattoos like old ladies kept Sweet'N Low. Janine could barely remember what Maddie's arms looked like clean. They'd been friends for ages and sometimes, it was like years folded into paper fans; they could be smoothed out and linear or they could crunch together and whip the heat from her face like they were children all over again. In that moment, she might as well have worn rainbow knee-highs and walked in the room with chocolate on her chin. Funny how you can still see the child.

Janine loved her in a way.

Usually in a haze of boxed wine, she'd ask Maddie the question: "How could Mom have baked that chocolate pie knowing she had her suitcase in the car?"

"Fuck her," Maddie'd say. "Maybe she didn't know. Maybe it was just spur of the moment. Besides, anyone can bake a pie. It's called Betty fucking Crocker."

Janine held that memory with soft hands. Chocolate pie on her day of days. It had been and would always be her favorite birthday; she ripped through box after box, flinging ribbon like a mad girl, before trying to climb the dogwood in her sailor dress and with Maddie's help, building a shelter out of the yellow plastic table cloth by heaving it over the swing set. She remembered the feel of wet grass on the back of her legs, the tickle of insects crawling beneath her. Her dad had pushed a bucket of flashlights and art supplies under the tent some time before the light faded; they had stayed out there for hours creating their own bohemia, even if it was a bit damp for construction paper. They hung drawings of houses, birds, and winter trees—sticking their pens and crayons through the plastic like nails through drywall. Maddie ripped up a picture of her house and glued it back together on a piece of poster board, leaving bits of white showing through. They tied silk scraps to the swing set. They twisted the chains, spinning in their own admiration, silk trailing beneath them. When they went inside, Janine's mother had gone to bed early with one of her headaches.

The next morning, her mother was gone.

A Wanda Jackson tune comes on the jukebox. It's barely loud enough to hear, but Janine knows it's the one about a mean man, and the beat gets in her. She'd sung it once, years ago. Celia and Maddie had told her she had the rasp and the sass to pull it off, but she had faked the lyrics in spots. It was before the store, before the economy went to hell. She and Maddie were still working the makeup counter in Belk's together. Maddie was still married to Jimmy then, and Janine had a steady girlfriend for once. Celia. Maddie had said they didn't fit; Celia was like a blonde cocker spaniel, with long waves caressing her limbs.

Celia smelled like bug spray and honeysuckle, though she had said they didn't have honeysuckle at the nursery where she worked—that Janine didn't understand flowers. They only made it through the end of summer. Janine had started to read a book about lilies on lunch breaks, folding pages down when the line drawings struck her. She thought if she could talk about the pistils of Asiatics it would matter.

They met while Janine had been brushing shadow on a bent woman's brows. When they made eye contact over a slope of white hair, Janine had pictured her head nuzzled in Celia's frail collarbone, pulling at the neck of her shirt, placing her hand there. She should have known better. The heat had been too high and she had scorched the finish. She had grasped her like a kid would a firefly, its guts squished between her fingers, still glowing, still disgusted with herself three years later. Celia made her want to strip the black dye from her hair and transform into a California girl with memories of cliffside oceans and walking on boardwalks—sea air, not stiff fabric, in her skin. Celia had left town soon after Janine asked if they could get a place together. Maddie had pulled her up, made her sit on the edge of the bathtub, told her to chew up two of her Xanax and go to bed. Janine had longed for that sweep of blur washing over her for days.

But Janine caught her breath and remained on the east side of town—the neighborhood her dad had hated. Left behind, she began to cultivate distaste for azaleas. She'd walk past the blooming bushes on her way into the mall. Hot pink. White. Soft pink. These colors started to annoy her. She thought of weed killer. Her dad in the summer fighting dandelions because he thought that's what he was supposed to do. She thought she'd like to see shrubbery like something from a Tim Burton movie, dark and twisting in unnatural poses. She'd thought of what they'd look like turned to metal, collecting snow.

That night—the night she turned her mouth into a rockabilly queen's, twisted and provocative and sore—had been legendary. Jimmy had even pushed a few tables against the wall and twirled Maddie, her killer calves popping in her Mary Janes. The owner didn't mind when he flung her into a table, sending canned tallboys to the floor because he and Jimmy had come up together. He threw a handful of rags at them, told them to get to it. Celia had joined them after a song or two until she got too dizzy to continue. Janine had told her to put her foot on the floor as they passed out that night; to keep the room from spinning, she had said, putting her hand on her belly, whimpering a little as she drifted off.

Janine mouths the words to Maddie, holds both arms out to her in a mock serenade.

"That bathroom never has paper towels," Maddie says.

"You should say something to Brian," Janine says, dropping her arms.

"There's not much point. It's me and my crappy luck. Never anything to wipe my hands with."

"Little Miss Sunshine," Janine says, unrolling the silverware and putting the paper napkin in her lap. "I went ahead and ordered."

"Pabst?"

"Yeah, I figured that was about all we could afford, beer-wise. Got us pickles and burgers to eat."

"No joke. Look at this," she says, lifting her arm up over her head. She sticks her fingers in a hole at her armpit. "This shirt's had it, but I can't really spend any money on new winter clothes right now. I got a fifty-dollar gift card to Marshall's for Christmas, but I had to use that on boots. My old ones started to split at the sole. I sat there one night with crazy glue trying to fix them and I thought to myself, this is what my life has become. No husband. No kids. No real job. A one-bedroom apartment next to a creek that floods and shoes that could star in their own sad puppet show."

"Tell me about it." She slides her clogs off. "Look under the table." Janine wiggles her big toe that's poking through a hole in her sock. The beer arrives just in time.

Maddie pours with a shaky hand. "It's too heady," Janine says. "Jimmy would give me so much shit for that."

"You ever hear from him anymore?"

"Not since he moved in with that woman," Maddie says, rocking her knife back and forth between her pointer and middle fingers.

"I know it's been a while but it's still weird he's not around. That it's just us again. It all comes back to us."

"You ever think we're the only ones that can stand each other?" Maddie asks, now smacking her palm with the flat side of the knife.

"Sometimes," Janine says. "Scary, huh?"

"Is that Marvin Gaye playing now?"

"Sounds like him. I don't know that song, though," Janine says, looking toward the jukebox.

"Jimmy used to play a lot of Marvin and Curtis," Maddie says, cracking her back by holding onto the table and twisting.

Janine wrinkles her nose when Maddie's back pops. "Strange coming from a punk and hardcore guy."

"He was a total music snob, though; don't you remember his record collection?"

"Yeah, I do. I just always thought it was a weird one." Janine takes the knife from Maddie and places it back on the table.

"I guess he wasn't so hardcore after all," Maddie says, running her finger over the condensation on her glass. "Look where he's living."

"He's certainly moved up in the world. What do you suppose the square footage of that house is?" Janine asks.

"Has to be at least 2,500, more if you count the garage. Never thought he'd be a kept man."

"Isn't he still working at Milestone?"

They reach for their glasses at the same time.

"Not more than part-time. He probably just stays for the discount, so he can keep collecting records."

The drums kick up hard and strong. Brian turns the volume up. Maddie and Janine finish their pitcher in record time. Maddie shakes her shoulders. Janine taps her foot. They look at each other and sing quietly.

"You gotta love Iggy Pop," Janine says.

"Fuck anything else," Maddie says.

"You girls need another?" Brian asks.

They nod and keep singing.

Everyone is back from their holiday trips so now Maddie only has two Pomeranians she walks regularly. The extra work dried up too quickly and what she earns from her 97-year-old client doesn't amount to more than forty dollars a day. Rachael Ray might be able to make that work, but Maddie recently moved into a ground-floor apartment in a community known both for being named after cheap cigarettes and being built on a flood-plain. They've known a lot of people over the years who have lived at Vantage Apartments and lost most of their belongings. One of Maddie's exes even lost his old Saab to the creek. It comes up too fast; flash floods move through and take out the garbage, as Janine's dad would say. It's just across Seventh Street from Gri-er Heights, a once relatively affluent segregated neighborhood built in the Jim Crow years, but the homes have fallen into dis-repair since the '70s. Maddie had railed about the apartments' name when she moved in: "Vantage, my ass," she'd said.

When the song's over, Janine goes quiet. She's thinking of the Dutch girl quilt her grandma gave her and how nice it'll feel piled up on top of her comforter tonight. She keeps the thermostat set on 65 in winter. She'll kiss the corner where her grandma em-broidered "For Janine 1982." "You hear from your mother lately?"

"She came by right after I moved in. She cried when she saw my place, asked me wasn't there anything I could do to win Jim-my back. She's psycho."

"She just worries about you, I guess." Janine shakes some salt onto her palm, licks it.

"She can't stand the fact that I'm divorced, broke, messy, and had a bottle of gin on my counter." Maddie picks strands of Po-meranian fur off her skirt, bitching about being too dumb to stop wearing velvet. Janine shakes her head to herself, wonders if

Maddie will ever pull herself out of her own storm drain.

Their waitress comes from behind Janine, says, "I got you, girls," setting their second pitcher and steaming food on the table.

Janine picks up her burger with both hands. Chili drips out.

"Slow asses," Maddie says. "There's hardly even anyone in here."

Janine covers her mouth, chewing, and says, "No kidding. Where is everybody?"

"Guess everyone's still recovering from the holidays. Plus, we're sort of here for the old ladybird special," she says, eyes shifting toward a couple who wear the same Florida Gator sweatshirts, one orange, one blue.

Maddie leans in for a bite of her burger. Janine watches the top of her head, notices white flecks along her part, which is straight down the middle, like always.

Maddie fills their glasses, salts her fried pickles, and in typical Maddie fashion proclaims, "Come March I'm out of here."

"Where to this time? California? Let me guess, San Francisco?"

"What in Jesus fuck would I want with the demented hippie fags in San Francisco?" Maddie asks. "Besides, I couldn't afford to live there."

"Hey," Janine says, "I don't know, you know us gays and our dogs. You could make some real money. I bet a couple of queens would even hire you to come spoon-feed their old bitches named Freddie and Mercury."

"People and their dogs," she says. "Cats are easier, less needy. They're like one-night stands you pick up in places like this, too sunk in their own drama to give a shit about yours," Maddie says. "Just like Flüeffer." Her head dips.

"So where are you planning on going exactly? You've left before. And what about your lease—didn't you sign a year?"

"Well, before, I was always following a guy. This time I'm just going. I think Pittsburgh, maybe. I know a girl up there from

New York who can probably get me a job. A real job, in an office," she says, dunking a pickle in ranch dressing. "I'd walk away from the lease for an eight-to-five. I mean, who gives a shit about that mildewed rat trap?"

"Pittsburgh?" Janine asks, "Who in holy hell would want to go to Pittsburgh?"

"I don't know," Maddie says, "Pittsburgh's pretty cool. At least it has more of an arts scene than Charlotte does. I just have to get out of the South, do something different. Everything's polluted here. Jimmy. The booze. The trees. The soul-scorching heat. I think I'm losing my shit."

"I don't know if you've noticed, but it's winter."

"Yeah, today it is, but next week it'll be in the sixties. Just watch. I can't tell who I'm supposed to be in this weather. I miss Chicago. It was ass-biting cold, and I knew to wear everything I owned. It didn't matter what I looked like under all those layers," Maddie says, putting her napkin on top of her basket. "Here, I'm just too exposed."

"Let's get the check," Janine says. "You're full of cheap beer and turning sour. Should we just walk back to your place? Come on, let's get your coat on." Janine takes her coat, holding it by its shoulders. "This coat," she says, rubbing her fingers together, "How can you stand it? The fabric is worse than the brocade on that gold chaise grandma used to have in her formal living room."

They walk with few words. Maddie trips over the sidewalk, recovers. Lately, Maddie spends her days smoking pot and watching old movies. Worrying about rain. When she watched *Sunset Boulevard* for the tenth time in a month, she thought maybe she should get out of the house more, so she had called Janine. Over the holidays, she had grown attached to the light her mini purple tree gave off, and she hadn't taken it down; she barely turned on anything aside from the tree and the television anymore. She had recently painted her coffee table black with an oil-based paint; it stayed sticky. Flüeffer, Maddie's friendly stoop cat, had become her closest companion. He had come by the patio the day she had painted the table and stuck his paw on the lid; for a few days afterward he was always trying to shake leaves and debris off. Now, he would look at her cockeyed from the hood of a neighbor's truck, at least until the rain started and his wet face drooped in her back window, begging to come inside. But he still picked at the hardened paint in his paw and threw her abrasive looks as he lay three feet away from her on the couch. Maddie thought he was judging her for her lifestyle. Janine thought that was an awful lot of judgment to put on a cat.

As they walk back to Maddie's, they move closer together in the chill of the January night, their limbs holding steady, if thin. Janine looks at the overcast sky, smells cold rain, and wonders what it would be like to live in Pittsburgh. Maybe Celia's been there. Maybe she's seen the steel jutting from the hills over the rivers, the retaining walls, the floods, the crazy winding of the streets that would make her sensitive stomach ill at every turn. She has to stop this. So does Maddie. Janine thinks about a customer named Linda who has been in the store three times in two weeks; she asks a lot of questions about sofa construction. Linda wants eight-way hand-tied. Linda has a good eye for line, for symmetry. A sturdy collarbone holding up a green tweed coat. Janine thinks maybe she should give her a chance. Five years is too long to pine.

Purple tree light seeps through the blinds, making Maddie's front window look exactly like the window of a person who stays inside too much, smoking pot and watching old movies. Janine wants to brush Maddie's hair and take her for walks. Make sure she eats and stand from a distance watching her progress, but she knows she can't. She can only walk her home.

"Where are your keys?" she asks, steadying Maddie with a hand to her back.

"My pocket," Maddie says, reaching in.

Inside, Janine turns on the television and a lamp by the back door, where Flüeffer is waiting. She lets him in, and runs her hand down his back; his tail shoots up like a flag. The space is cramped with litter. Yogurt cups sit empty on the coffee table that everything sticks to. Heeled shoes and a pair of rhinestone flip-flops wait by the back door. Maddie'd worn those at her wedding, saying even though it was a beach wedding and no one would see her feet, she needed a little sparkle down there. Don't we all? Janine had thought. Maddie drops onto the couch, tucking her toes in between the cushions, and propping her head on the high, tufted arm. She needs to have the upholstery cleaned. Pot ash and cat fur, dried specks of gin and lime dot the velvet. Janine cleans the kitchen counter and loads the dishwasher. There's no soap, so she runs the load on high temperature.

"You need dishwasher detergent," she calls from the kitchen.

"Among other things," Maddie says.

Maddie flips back and forth between VH1 Classic and AMC. She lingers on a movie about a mental institution. Maddie's digging a moat again, distancing herself. Janine can see she has done her no good. Maddie says people are too much like Flüeffer; she says Janine comes through in her way, but sparsely. She often talks about how quiet things have been in the year since Jimmy left. He'd left his leather jacket in her coat closet at the old place. She wears it occasionally, though the arms come to her fingertips. Maddie likes to use that word—*sparse*. Maddie could be unreachable. Jimmy had left her for a woman with a five-year-old who lived on the same street as the Pomeranians. Maddie tried to walk them in the opposite direction, but sometimes she'd see them driving past her in a brown Volvo. A Volvo, for fuck's sake! Inevitably, the female, a sable-coat named Charla Mae, would take a crap about the same time so Maddie would lean down, her arm in a glove-shaped trash bag, capturing the steam and the smell, before brushing her hair out of her face with the other hand.

Janine thinks it must be the coldness of Steeltown that sounds good to Maddie. Alfred Hitchcock good. She could walk through the grit and the snow feeling like it matched. Charlotte isn't a town to be depressed in. It is a town to settle down and buy stuff in. Maddie had tried that once before and certainly couldn't do it walking dogs or doing makeovers for the wives of athletes and bankers, or marrying a guy named Jimmy who wanted her to "move more in bed." It is a town to have Pomeranians and Volvos in. To tease your hair in. Move to the south side. Have babies. Fix meals. Be quiet. Janine knows Maddie wants her to go to Pittsburgh, too, but Maddie won't ask. Janine also knows neither of them is likely to leave.

Janine takes her coat off, places it on the back of the chair by the door, and sits down with a sigh. Maddie has a perfect blank stare; she can blink hard and remove herself.

"Pittsburgh?" Janine asks.

Maddie looks at the ceiling. "Pittsburgh," she says.

"Why don't you just come to work with me at the store?"

"Because I fucking love furniture so much. Clearly," she says, gesturing at the room.

"But we had fun at Belk's, playing in makeup," Janine says. "Remember when we used to get in canned air fights?"

Maddie laughs, "Yeah, and the time I was blowing the excess off the pressed powder display and one of the samples was too loose? That shit flew everywhere. In my mouth. Up my nose. Up your nose."

"Yeah," Janine says, making a space in the clutter for her feet, "What about those theme parties? That time we both wore white wigs with delphinium stuck in them?"

"April in Paris?" she asked. "I could rock a backless shirt then. All it had was two strings, remember?"

"You told me to tie them tight so you wouldn't flop around," Janine says.

The rain starts hard and fast, sounding like marbles dropping on glass. "You get any floods yet?" Janine asks.

"Not yet," she says. "But looks like tonight's a possibility. Better start stacking shit on the counter."

"What about the sofa? The upholstery?"

"Got any inflatable furniture at the store?" she asks, pulling her low-slung pants up as she stands. Janine thinks of her seventh birthday, that tablecloth—the sweet, closed-off, grassy smell. The light behind the yellow. Maddie's round face and self-inflicted haircut. The damp paper.

"Better unplug this," Janine says, moving the tree to the top of the fridge.

"Maybe we should call your dad," Maddie says.

"He's sleeping by now. I'll call tomorrow."

"Will you stay?" Maddie asks.

"Let's go sleep at the store," she says. "I don't want to just sit here, waiting for creek water. You can pick any bed you want."

At the store, they light candles and set them on the night-stands next to the four-poster. They fold the covers back together. Maddie has to sleep farther from the door. Janine crawls in on the right, closer to the register.

"Are those rosemary candles?" Maddie asks, staring up at the muslin.

"Yeah, I bought a ton of them," Janine says, turning to her side, looking toward the door.

Lightning strikes less. The storm lets up. They don't say good-night. They drift off, the candles still burning in their glass jars, turning all liquid except those bits on the edge that cling. Janine wakes in a panic near dawn, the room sick with rosemary, and blows them out. As she lies back down, she thinks of the cold, wet ahead. The rummaging. The salvaging. The awful smell of mildew.

Buddy and Lurch

Jeremy looked at Letty like she was a tree or a limb, something alive, but weathered. A branch hanging loose, bark coming undone, piled up around her like she was shooting a big-ass machine gun, shells everywhere. At least, that's what she guessed since he hadn't been coming home from the road much lately.

She walked past this pine every day. The top had broken off last time the wind came up and its western half looked like it was running from something, limbs all twisted back around, almost hugging itself for want of comfort.

With a little whiskey in her morning coffee, Letty moved easier through her days. But she loved Buddy and their twelve-year-old pug, Lurch, to bits and couldn't stand the thought of life without them. She repeated their names to herself on her walks, Buddy and Lurch, until it started to sound in her head like some kind of verb that meant something, making her gut hurt, burning at a low temperature.

Lurch wasn't much into walking since his knees started clicking out of socket and Letty knew it was only a matter of time. She had it in mind to leave after Lurch, as long as Buddy got into a good college. Buddy and Lurch.

By the time she turned forty-six, her face had started to feel foreign to her, unfamiliar in a way, like hearing someone in pain cry out in Italian. Her face was *romanesco* for tired and fed up and neglected. Her words hovered out of reach; something like *stanco e di alimentato in su*, but that could have translated to "having eaten." Only a piece of her Nonna's native language lingered in her mind, most of it food-related.

When Letty put her palm against the tree's trunk every day before turning back, she knew one day it'd all be over and done. She'd stop waiting and do something for once. Save up enough to get back to Rome, Nonna's Navona, smoke where she smoked on Bernini's Fountain of the *Quattro Fiumi*, eat whole fish and spaghetti *cacio e pepe* at Antica Taverna. One day, Letty would smell the world from behind a garlic and lemon-infused veil.

It wasn't until Jeremy had been gone nine days this stretch that she got the idea to cut the tree down.

At 2:36 A.M., she woke, body slicked over not only from the flannel, but hormones, too. She sat straight up, scooped Lurch under his front paws and said, "Booger, Mama's got it. I'm gonna cut that old pine down." Lurch snorted and wriggled out of her arms to reclaim his spot at the foot of the bed.

Jeremy had a chainsaw. The tree wasn't so big. She knew deep in her belly pain that the tree was done for anyway. Buddy and Lurch.

In her plaid pajamas and bear slippers, she grabbed Jeremy's headlamp from the garage and snapped on some safety goggles. True, she'd never worked the thing before, but she had been with Jeremy at Home Depot when he bought it. As she looked at green paint samples for the bathroom, she heard the salesclerk say it had almost a pound of horsepower per engine weight.

When Letty pulled the cord, it felt like that time Jeremy had made her fire the double-barrel, nearly knocking her on her ass, but she got ahold of it, felt the vibrations clear through her body. Even the bear claws shook. Buddy and Lurch.

Buddy hadn't always taken it easy on her. He blamed her for their troubles—the times when they only had chicken wings to eat and Goodwill clothes. "You couldn't have married someone who gave a damn?" he'd ask as he slammed his bedroom door and cranked up Iron Maiden. "Can't you do more than sell cheap makeup to divorcees? Didn't you want more out of life, Ma?"

For a time, Letty wondered if Buddy would ever understand how hard it had been with just her GED. She couldn't really fault him though, for saying the shit she conjured up all on her own. Things didn't start to change between them until he'd found her passed out next to their Civic. She wouldn't let him take her to the hospital, told him it was just anxiety, but she'd watched his movements alter as he dabbed peroxide on her abrasions and bandaged them up.

Now and then these days, Buddy borrowed the car to pick up Captain D's for dinner, just to give her a break. Buddy and Lurch.

Streetlights flickered as she took her usual route zigzagging through her neighborhood. She thought someone, Ms. Peabody maybe, who stayed up to all hours online shopping, would instinctively come out to stop her. Buddy and Lurch.

At the tree, Letty held the chainsaw with two hands. She tested it out on the scraggy lower limbs. Quick zipping, a momentary resistance and she was almost spun around by the force of it cutting through. She clenched her teeth and bore down hard near the base.

Buddy and Lurch.

GETTING BY WITH SOUND

D ad only read well enough to follow traffic signs and, sometimes, write a check. Between the army and Mother, he got
by, but when I was a boy, I'd squish next to him in his recliner,
a Tolkien book in my hand. First it was *The Hobbit*, then each
of the *Lord of the Rings* books. There I'd sit, my legs sometimes
sticking to his, my fingers following the words as I tried to get
him to say them with me.

"See, there," I'd say, "'Riv-en-dell' like 'riv-er.' It's where the
elves live." I had wanted to teach him, was desperate to help,
partly out of embarrassment for him but mostly for me. I'd see
him struggle when we went to the hardware store. He knew how
to grow things, what he needed, but he couldn't tell what was
what because the words were skeletons. He knew his brands, but
if they changed the packaging, he'd get lost; his eyes would go
loose.

He'd stand there a minute, point at the new green bag, "That
peat moss?" he'd ask, patting the bulky square. "Smells like it."

"That's peat," I'd say about the time he stuck his pocketknife
through the plastic.

Up in his leather recliner, with me as his teacher, his jaw would
stick behind his stubble. I'd see his muscle pumping and think he
was telling me something, but wasn't real sure what that might
be. When he got that way, sometimes I'd ask him to tell stories
about the war—the smells were what he liked to talk about the
most, so when I'd come up on those kind of sense words, I'd put
a little more oomph in it.

When I read the description of Smaug, he leaned back, closed
his eyes, and said, "Mmmm hmmm. I bet he smelled like sulfur."

"What does sulfur smell like?" I asked, looking up from the
book.

"Like matches," he said. "Like death. It has a sound too, that singe and scrape. Bones and splinters. Sand and falling. Like my buddy's hair burning," he said, putting me on the floor and stretching his legs. "Sounds like your writer has seen combat."

"How can you tell?" I asked, tossing the book back in the milk crate, which was full of our paraphernalia—his water-damaged deck of cards and a bag of Circus Peanuts; the books and a cap gun and its ammo, mine.

Back then, I knew he'd like the same books as me if I could just get him reading, but he said he was content to "set and listen," rather than read himself; he liked the way my eyes bulged in spots and how my face transformed with the words. He let me read to him right up until he died, though I probably just washed into the white noise of the respirator by the end of it. Mother had gone fast, plowed down years ago by a dump truck when she made an illegal U-turn, but my father took longer when his time come up—had a four-month postscript to a stroke he would've just as soon torched. I had suctioned off bits of dried saliva in the corners of his mouth and come away with doubt over my bones. There are times dying takes too long.

But back then, when we weren't knee-deep in epics of orc versus elf, we walked his property. Those were the things he liked to do. Listen to stories, walk, and admire the scent of his gardenias, the feel of their waxy leaves and petals. He used to pick them for my mother, and she always kept them on the windowsill in the kitchen. They were beautiful until the petals turned brown, but then the smell just grew sweeter. He liked to climb the hill at the back of the property. Not that it was a lot of land at three-quarters of an acre but it was big enough to get him winded in his old age. He had made the property thick with plants—hostas in the shade, peonies and roses in the sun. He said they were for Mother, but I know he took pride in them just as much as she did. He pruned. She didn't. She spent more time in the little room sewing than she did outside. That's why she was otherworldly pale.

His pride was visible in the manicure of it all. He used to say the house was so white it made him glad he didn't die fighting Nazis in Holland. He had thought the last thing he'd see was snow and dirt and smoke, and the slush of his own blood. The sound of artillery scarring the land. He repainted the house every year, come June. Swore that would be the last thing he laid eyes on. He'd die listening to the sounds of his house settling. I don't think I'll ever get over the fact that he went out wishing for that view; eyes fogging over in a hospice room with motel art and the serenity prayer on the wall. I can only guess the last thing he saw was whatever fake tiles they put on the ceilings in offices and hospitals. The last thing he heard a slowing beep and the whirr of a breathing machine.

I should have taken him home.

The earth around back of the house is rooty, but dark and rich because of a couple hundred-year-old oaks Mom had saved from the chainsaw; he hadn't wanted anything obstructing the view of the house. He kept talking about cutting them down after she died. It was strange that they weren't the trees of my memory; they were taller, fuller, sure, but they'd grown a thick coat of lichen and were mostly green-bodied now. How they'd changed that much without me noticing over the years is beyond me. On our walks, Dad would point out a sprout that had come up from the ground, tighten the twine around a tomato plant, put his knees to the ground and lean in for a whiff. He said the smell of the peat moss and compost stuck in his soul. The rustle of the leaves seemed like fingertips on his shoulders, kneading away the past. He always had his hand on something living. "You have to watch that you don't overwater the tomatoes," he'd say, "you'll get root rot." He'd stick his fingers in the dirt to feel for water, talk about the sweetness of squash blossoms. Sometimes, he'd pull a radish right out of the ground, thump the dirt off, and eat it without a thought. Most times I was preoccupied with how to defend the neighbor girl from the menace of goblins, fighting the air behind her with my cardboard sword. If I could learn to climb the fence in one sweeping, springing maneuver, I thought,

I could reach her window in time. Dumb kid. Too involved in fantasy for my own good, weapons and valiance stuck in my head like a stutter.

Ever since Dad passed, when I rubbed my hands, I saw his. Thick canvas hands. Nails like concrete. Didn't even need gloves. Mine were thinner, but I hadn't got the years he had yet. Laying vinyl made mine arc in ways I never figured. I had a hump over my thumb's knuckle; my pinky had a deep crevice on the outer edge. Though the marks that really begged questioning had nothing to do with work. They had to do with a sliding glass door and my ex-wife, Loretta. Still, I knew my hands ached in the same spots his did, and there I sat on the same porch with four beers after a long day of working them. Dad would roll over in his grave if he saw that I had let the paint start flaking. The bushes needed trimming, too. I didn't much care since I'd never planned on moving in his place anyway. I only did it to take care of him while he was sick; now the place belonged to me free and clear, and it seemed stupid to leave and make things worse on myself financially. The truth was I couldn't get over his death while I lived in his house— in the town and neighborhood I'd always planned to leave. It was too sculpted, if you ask me. I shouldn't have sold my own house. I'd loved that little ranch. It was new when Loretta and I bought it when she was pregnant with Janine. We'd decorated it contemporary. I sold all the chrome and glass at a yard sale. Most of the rest of it I'd donated. I took the glider with its crisp white frame and blue leather cushions. I had Janine's old bedroom furniture out in the garage with the Rubbermaid boxes of stuffed animals and masks she'd left with me. Her roller skates. Janine also made me keep the clothes her grandma had made for her. Her outfits were piled neatly, one on top of the other, in several of the longer Rubbermaids. It sure had been help, those clothes. I could barely afford to clothe the two of us back then. Though I do wish she'd come take her junk to her own house so I could park my truck in there.

Three beers in, I played the message Loretta left me earlier.

Said she wanted to come by that afternoon to talk about Janine. I knew she had just come out of the closet to Loretta, and I took from the way her voice seemed to be on fast forward that she wasn't handling the news so well. She ran at the mouth like the harpy I remembered. I could see her hair shaking like a whip. I pressed stop before it was over, called her back, said come on if you're coming.

I can hate the woman. The way she left. I could see it coming before she did, but leaving a heavy metal handyman with a seven-year-old girl was some kind of behavior for a woman. For years, I'd pictured her busted up and crying in damp motel rooms over what she'd done. But I doubt that ever happened. She probably had the time of her life on the road.

Sometimes, I still miss her. All these years later. I remember her face at the Judas Priest concert, angry and pale, raising her fist, and banging her head like a man. The way her hips had shape even though she was too thin. She's a smashed down, watery version of that girl now. Beat to hell. By me and Janine and another two marriages afterwards. It was stupid of me to think being a mama would quiet her demons; even baby smells and toddler ringlets weren't enough.

I hear gravity and hard living's done a number on Loretta. Janine said she wanted to smooth her eye skin when she saw her, to run her thumbs over the under part of her eye, pressing lightly and pushing outward. I told her I'd like to be there if she ever tries that. The rage I once felt toward Loretta had fallen away for me most days, but Janine just couldn't let go of the confusion, the abandonment, the fact that I had tried to fix her hair, and had done it badly. The whole phantom limb of the situation was what got me.

With a breeze blowing, I wondered how Loretta didn't know about Janine; to me, she had always shown signs. She never saw boys. Her eyes would follow mine across the neck of her teenage cousin, even as a youngster. She saw that butterfly tattoo move the same way I did. The trouble with Loretta was that she didn't pay attention to the world right in front of her. She didn't see me, seeing her back then. A glaring billboard of infidelity. She hadn't seen the desperation that grew with my stomach, or the sadness I stacked in Ursula Le Guin books in the corner of the living room, but I could see her plain as day when she switched to a Chicago T-shirt, how she tried too hard with Janine. Like she was shooting for Lord of the Mothers—one mother to rule them all. I had taken to burping beer foam, and waiting for the inevitable. And she didn't see Janine now. I couldn't imagine what good she thought it would do talking to me about it.

Loretta was probably doing one of two things; she was either blaming herself for Janine being gay because she left us and wanted to be let off the hook, or she was blaming me for taking little Janine to work and dressing her in tiny Slayer T-shirts or some bull. Like the hammers had somehow soaked into her blood and couldn't get flushed out. Like there was some kind of right way and wrong way to be in the world.

Rachel and Lucille came out on the porch next door, waved hello. They'd sometimes bring supper over for me after Dad died, but they didn't like me drinking. They eyed me like only old Southern women can. I covered my mouth to burp, ignoring them.

Janine needed to get out of Dodge. It would be harder for her here. Some redneck would see her with a woman and, at the very least, preach to her about God hating dykes. I used to get the same thing because of my long hair. At school, the good old boys never hesitated to rain down a "faggot" or two with the bottles they threw. In their eyes, being into books and Aerosmith and having long hair made some kind of surefire gay soup out of me. It would be the same story for Janine. If I could put down my beer, spread my chest in front of her, and wrap her in a fatherly cloak, I would. But I couldn't hide her, and I knew I shouldn't want to.

About the time I had fidgeted the tab off the can and lined it up with the other three, Loretta pulled up in her Civic, silver, like the streaks in her hair. She looked wild, her hands banging against her thighs as she came up the walk.

"Trees are starting to turn," she said, biting at a hangnail.

"What's with the fidgeting? Can I get you a beer, Loretta?"

"Nah, but I'll take a Diet Coke, if you got one," she said, plopping down on the top step.

When she spoke, I had a strong urge to go inside, kick the door shut, lock it, and leave her there wondering where I'd gone. Let her get hysterical like I had so many times before. She was a lot to handle, that woman. But I poured her diet soda in a plastic cup and tried to understand where she was coming from.

"Thanks," she said, "What are we going to do?"

"About what?" I asked.

"Janine," she said, putting the cup down beside her, "What do you think?"

I leaned against the railing, folded my arms. "Well, what is it you think can be done?"

"I don't know, but what are people going to say? Isn't it enough with all we went through? With the divorces. Now everyone's going to think I'm a bad mother."

"So, what, you think you can dodge that boulder?"

"Well, how come you seem so calm about it, Hardy? You two. I swear. Always against me," she said, pulling her hair up into a high ponytail. It made her look older. I felt the same urge to push on her face that Janine did, and despite all she put me through, to put my lips on hers.

"I don't know. I guess it ain't much of a surprise. She's never really been boy crazy like you and your sisters were, coming up. You three were machine-gun girlfriends—hell, wives, for that matter. Weren't boys camping out on your stoop by the time you were twelve?"

"Well, I guess I missed that," she said.

"I guess you did," I said. "What makes you think you can change anyone, Loretta? Of all people?"

"I'm just tired of the talk," she said. "There's never any room for difference around here. You know that as well as anybody. If people like us aren't careful, the Bible Belt will strangle us."

"I hear you, but, maybe, just maybe, you should start worrying more about yourself. She's grown now, you know. And you're gonna lose any chance you had at being a mom if you don't calm the hell down and swallow this easier than you do everything else." I sat down next to her. "Just settle down. So she likes women. What difference does that make? She's going to love the wrong people no matter what. That's how it works, right? Just look at us. Look at yourself."

She got quiet. Our breathing and movements began to synch. She'd tap her foot after I started swinging mine. She'd lean up. I'd lean up. We waited for someone to speak. I saw her feet in those boots, worn down to stubs of the heels they used to be, the buckle no longer silver, now turned copper. Those heels were the first thing I'd seen that time I came home to her passed out next to the dining table. I'd come up the back porch, and there she was on the other side of the sliding glass window, face down. Not answering. I banged on the door with my keys. Screamed her name until it had no meaning. Until I ran out of breath. Until the moment I knew we were flat out lost. To each other. Maybe even to the whole world. For Loretta, there was too much overlap. The skins of her conquered beloveds hung over each other like pelts, but the whole lot of us were unable to dry properly and we all rotted instead of curing. I took a log off the stack of firewood we kept on the porch and smashed the glass to get to her. It spat shards, which is how I got my hand so mangled up. That night I drove us both, one-handed, to the hospital. She got her stomach pumped. I got seventeen stitches. Mother came over to watch Janine, helped me get Loretta in the car. She had wrapped my hand up in one of our black towels so we wouldn't be able to see the stain. "Well, there's no sense in ruining a perfectly good towel," she had said and then, when we shoveled Loretta in the car, "Her face is swollen. I won't ask what's going on."

"Good, Ma," I had said. "Don't. Just take care of Janine. I

doubt she'll wake up but just in case, tell her we decided to go out dancing."

Loretta's face was thin now, angular. I rubbed my hands and Loretta said, "I was real sorry to hear about your old man."

She touched my thumb with hers.

"Thanks," I said, "I thought you'd come to the funeral. He always did like you. Said he never saw a woman so different from his own—so much spit, so little perfume."

"The old man and I saw eye-to-eye. Understood each other. You and your mother."

"Me and my mother what?" I asked as I stood to close and lock the front door.

"You're just alike. Same judgment. Same blue-gray, daydreaming eyes rolling around in your head."

"I don't see it," I said. "She was content here. Once Janine came along and after she retired anyway." I said I couldn't believe it had been so long since she'd died. Janine was twelve at the time; my mother had just dropped her off, loaded down with bags of Christmas presents. She was on her way home when her Oldsmobile was T-boned on Independence Boulevard. Her sudden death had sucked the air out of every room. Dad didn't come inside much after that and I had my hands full with a grieving child.

Poor girl had already lost one mother. That year Janine passed out all the boxes her grandma had helped her wrap, her sweet eyes still swollen from crying. She patted each one as if she were patting her grandma's bouffant. Like the hair, none of us moved. When she was finished, we piled boxes around her so high she had had to quarry her way through them. We tried to forget our grief and cure Janine's by spoiling her.

But there was no sound of joy that morning.

I had opened my gift certificate to K & W Cafeteria and the card Mom had never had the chance to sign and dropped them in a gift bag full of wool socks my dad had given me. Janine examined each sweater, the makeup kit, and the rhinestone Guess jeans, as though she were looking at my mother's face. Janine's hands were more gentle than I'd ever seen them, sticking under the taped folds. She wouldn't open her own gift from Mom. She left it sitting on top of her twelve-inch TV I'd gotten for her until her birthday in June. It sat there, a beacon in red foil. It was a vintage drawing from a sewing pattern Mom had saved from her childhood; she'd placed it in a simple silver frame. The sketch was filled with watery color that barely stayed inside the rough outline of the fitted skirt, blazer, and pillbox hat. I noticed the woman's trim ankles and pumps, her closed eyes. It hangs above the register in Janine's store to this day.

Mom and I hadn't spent that much time together growing up. She worked hard at the mill and fed me three squares a day and collapsed on the sofa every night after dinner. She used to complain all the time about only getting five minutes for lunch and having to eat on her feet. Sitting down was real important once dinner was over. That's when Dad and I did most of our reading.

"Let's get out of here for a bit," I said. "You drive."

"Still doing the beer thing, then?" Loretta walked ahead of me to her car, got in, unlocked the passenger side from within.

"The ritual's what I have left of him."

"What about your books?" she asked.

"Well, those too," I said, pulling open the door with a jolt. "Door's sticking."

"Yeah, she's seen better days," she said. "Sorry for the smell."

"What is that, pea soup?"

"I honestly couldn't tell you," she said, laughing, "Where are we going?"

I wiped the foggy glass with my sleeve. She started the car and backed out without looking. We waved bye to Rachel and Lucille.

"Jesus, Loretta, pay attention."

"I knew nobody was coming," she said.

I turned the radio to 99.7 The Rock. Bon Jovi was on. She loved them so I left it alone, but I liked my rock heavier. Wished I'd picked up my Black Sabbath tape. Or AC/DC—we could agree on them at least. "Let's go to Pop's grave," I said. "He would've liked it if you'd come."

"Can we stop for a bag of Red Man? I'll leave it on the headstone."

"How Gaston County of you. That shit'll get rained on and petrify on Daddy's grave."

"Well," she said, "It would just be a gesture. I did love your daddy, and he loved that tobacco."

We stopped at the 7-Eleven on the way to the cemetery. She got tobacco; I got a bag of peanut M&M's and a Sprite to pass the time in the car so we didn't feel obligated to talk.

Mom and Dad were buried on what used to be the black side. It was cheaper. I followed a step or two behind her; she still remembered where Mom was buried, and I guess that gave me some kind of comfort—that she walked straight to the far side, by the sugar maple which would soon be taken over by the best red I'd ever seen. When we got to the graveside, she put the bag up against the stone, on Dad's side.

"Was it as bad as hers?" she asked.

"Quieter," I said. "Less wailing. Janine and I were the only ones sitting up under the tent. Had a military service, guns, and a flag, the whole nine." I sat down, Indian-style, and picked at the new weed growth around the edge of the stone. Ran my fingers over cold granite. She sat on the bench next to the tree. Janine had had it made, some carpenter friend of hers. It looked like it was carved out of one piece of walnut and stood out from the rest of the benches, smooth among a rough landscape. Loretta hugged her knees to her chest. She was cold; her nose turned pink at the end. She had chocolate in the corner of her mouth, but I didn't have the heart to tell her.

"I'm sorry I missed it," she said, hanging her head. "And for being wasted at your mother's."

"It's getting colder, smells like fall," I said. "You know, he didn't get to die at home."

"Not looking at the whiteness of the house?" she asked, rocking a little.

"No, in a damn hospital room."

"I hope I don't go out like that."

"Maybe we can strike a deal, look out for each other?" I asked, picking at the grass.

"You got it," she said. "I never did understand how he was going to die looking at the house, anyway. What did he want you to do, cart him out in the yard?"

"I believe he would've," I said. "It would have been better than rotting in that horrible room to the sound of my voice reading *A Game of Thrones.*"

"Go a little easier on yourself, Hardy. You did what you needed to. I'll bet hearing you read to him brought him peace, and surely ranked a close second behind staring at some old house you hadn't even painted." She crept up behind me; she crouched down, putting her hands on my ears. "Guess I should go easier on Janine, too," she said. "Your ears are cold." The traffic and the rustling muffled beneath her hands and I cried for the first time in months.

QUIET

A story hunkers under grass. Somewhere below or between Anthony's toes, words wriggle, words wake. Kittens mewl in the crawlspace, the sun, high and severe, makes our eyes water. Milky. I pinch my thumb and forefinger together, wanting to push their eyes open. Eight days old and they're half the size of his flat feet. Tortie. Torbie. Tabby.

We still taste cow-infused dirt, how mushroom caps caught in our jaws. Their grime comes back on most of us. Mary Theresa holds the banister, giggles in between heaves under a straw curtain of hair. Because I'm quiet, they decide I'm most capable. I walk to the pool hall to get grilled cheese sandwiches. Customers stare. Faces turn to ash. Tires squeal outside and I squint hard, hand the man a twenty, and walk away with the greasy bag. When I get back, Mary Theresa's still holding on; she grabs her right hand with the left to steady them both.

We eat on the porch sofa in silence, wiping mouths with our forearms.

Interior walls breathe in frantic puffs. Mary Theresa wants to see the attic. I follow Anthony's lower limbs. Loose calves and ankles, like someone has snipped them apart, and strung them back together with fishing line. Tonight, I will thread him to me. In my mind I have a needle the size of garden shears. Fabric woven from maple leaves and dandelion fluff. He pushes Mama Cat away as we pass. She groans, low, from her full belly. We climb thin steps. Mary Theresa misses one, almost falls, but a hand braces her, pushes. His hand. We settle around the attic opening, legs drawn in, settling on fiberglass, our skin pinking.

Anthony shows a child's artwork—it flakes when touched. Letters betray each other; the O in Mom is oafish. The Ds all lowercase. There's not enough light. With earth in my mouth, a kitten screams. Mama Cat trails to the cat door. Crates on our ribs. Car horns. I dig the lighter out of my pocket; it spits and catches. Mary Theresa passes me a wedding photo; I put corner to flame. It bubbles. Flares. It slips when it gets down to my fingertips, falling to the carpet. Extinguishes. My thumbnail, browned.

Words recede into mold.

Downstairs snarls and thuds. Anthony and I stand, get locked up, fall. Hips absorb shock, skin ripples. Mama Cat stands over me, her lip hanging open, dripping, victorious.

Back pulsing, I look for his toes to make the first stitch.

I Can't Do Much,
But I Can Bake a Pie

Some days I wish the universe would get on with it. The shit I've done and here I am walking around without a hitch. Tawni got hers. We'll never know if she did it on purpose or not. Then there's Rory, who lost his legs when he passed out on train tracks, probably daring Jay and Brandon to lie down with him. I still don't know about drummers. The singer for Blindness staged a regular cliché by falling into a nod he never came out of. Yet, here I am, somehow alive with a sister who still hasn't given up on me.

In her slip and heels, Brenna pokes her head in my room. "I've got the list ready. You want to meet for dinner first?" she asks, brushing her cheeks with powder.

"Chinese?"

"We just had Chinese Saturday." She leaves and returns dressed, fastening pearl earrings.

"You're asking me before I've had my coffee?"

"Let's go light," Brenna says, slapping her hips. "If we're baking, I need to cut calories somewhere."

"Yeah, you're starting to look like Miss Hassenfuss. But honestly, who cares?"

"Oh, God. I remember her. That hair. Cut like a man's and permed up right." Brenna runs her hand over her cropped hair and mutters something about three divorces, says, "I'm cooler than that."

"What time?"

"I'll be there around 5:30. I have to stay late for a parent-teacher conference."

"Sounds good," I say, kicking back the blankets. "Get out of here, already."

"You'll be okay on your own? Nice shirt."

"Kiss still rules. I'm fine. Now, get."

All else aside, we Helms sisters are known for stress baking. Funerals. Illness. Bad day at work, shitty haircut, another damn man, what have you. Sugar eases pain. Brenna is a pastry dough master. I have perfected a chocolate-hazelnut pie that is so creamy you'd swear I bake all the time. That pie is my one and only talent. Everything else turns out wrong. Cakes crumble. Brownies harden like stone. Brenna says I'm too lazy about measurements. Dorian is best at licking batter off spoons and cleaning, but she says someone has to do it, so we still let her.

Brenna has always been good at distracting me. Back in town, I'm hit square with all of it. Heavy memories clunk down from recesses of my brain I thought I'd killed off long ago. A month home and I haven't settled or made much progress with Janine. She's what it's all about. Maybe Gary a little bit, but I'm not even sure our marriage is worth saving. Seems like we both know separation means divorce. Gary seemed content in Asheville, but said it was time to do something about my guilt once and for all and brought my ass home to Brenna.

"You can't fix leaving," he said. "But you can work on now. Either way, I'm not bearing the brunt of your mistakes anymore. Don't you know you're a disaster, even sober? Talk to Hardy. Do something for Christ's sakes."

Step Nine: Own your previous role as queen bitch. Relinquish your crown.

Hardy and I had had a good talk about Janine a few weeks back, but I haven't heard from him since. Maybe I crossed the line when I touched his ears. Hardy always was a tender man, but he was still grieving for his dad and running in his own guilt hamster wheel, so maybe we weren't the best company for each other. Hardy used to toss and turn in his sleep, left the sheets twisted to hell in the morning. When Gary slept next to me, I evened out. He'd settle in on his back with one arm under his head and the other on his stomach and I swear he barely moved. To me, this was the manifestation of his stability. My whole past, present, and future are a lot to try to get to sleep with and a heap more to wake up to.

Over and over, I pick at the thread of me.

I still haven't mastered days off. Brenna's right to worry. Work kept my mind off it to a point. Even there, I marked time by how many Cokes or Snickers bars I sold. The best customers bought presents for newborns, but think about the size of a hospital and ratios of sick patients to newborns and you'll get swimmy-headed too. Most people came to buy *get well soon* balloons, a popular choice the spotted dog with a thermometer in his mouth and a cold pack on his head. That droopy-eyed bastard even showed up in my dreams.

How long you've been good doesn't matter.

Last night, this guy came in asking for NoDoz. I had seen him around for about a week. Good, if serious, cheekbones, high like Paul Newman. Between his bones and sandy coloring, he was easy to notice. "We don't sell speed at the hospital. You might try the Circle K across the street. We don't have cigarettes either."

"Bummer," he said.

"Right? So. Who are you and what are you in for?"

"Wife's in surgery. Exploratory. Her intestines. Still bleeding. They don't know what's wrong," he said with the door to the cooler swung open, staring into the rows of sodas and flavored waters like he'd never opened another cooler in his life. In the moment, I can see him at nine years old with a pocketful of change, a Rocket Pop and soda in his hand. In the past, he looks the same, but he still has the bright eyes of the pain-free.

"Maybe a couple of Cokes will help you stay awake or if you can't leave, I could go over on my break and get your NoDoz or Vivarin, or whatever."

"I'll just take this and get back." He put a generic soda and a Milky Way on the counter.

"That should hold you for a bit. $2.86."

"Cafeteria's cheaper though."

"But closed."

Night hours at the store were almost as bad as free time. I just try to fill increments of time. Make it through the next half hour. No figurine or box of candy was ever out of place. The customers weren't any different. People looked for something to do besides wait. We are antsy, chittering creatures if you think about it. Some of them smelled of booze. Some damp and greasy. When someone would come in for a *congratulations* balloon or bear, I'd talk them into gift baskets of stuffed bears or elephants and tiny pink or blue onesies and trashy magazines for the mom. I'd put in diaper cream and pacifiers. Things the mother probably already had. I loved the little socks that looked like ballet shoes. I wrapped the whole thing in plastic, tied a bow and bottle-shaped balloon around them, and turned ribbons to ringlets with my scissors.

Mr. Paul Newman came back forty-nine minutes later, not that I was counting. "Any word?" I asked, coming out from behind the counter.

"Nothing yet," he said. "I can't seem to stay awake up there. You'd think with all that's going on, I could at least do that for her." He picked up one of the pink bears.

"You can't help the fact that you're tired and overwhelmed. Maybe go a little easy on yourself." I knew that was some kind of preaching, but hell if it isn't easier to dole out advice than take it.

"It's been thirty-four years since my baby girl was born. Remember the '70s?" he asked, scratching the bear's ears.

"Barely."

"Now, she won't even come home from New York when her mother's in the hospital." He put the bear back on the shelf. I could see him just like Newman in *The Hustler*, holed up and drunk in a stranger's apartment. A year ago, I was that stranger. "You got kids?"

"None that would claim me. You sure you don't want me to run to the store?"

"Might as well let you, I guess. Can't leave. Can't stay awake."

"What floor you on?"

"Fifth floor, critical care."

"I'll take my break in about half an hour. I'll find you." He started to pull his wallet from his wrinkled khakis. "No, I got this," I said, grateful to be able to offer a man what he needed without judgment.

The last time I bought NoDoz I was out of money and looking for a cheap high. I crunched them up and snorted them in the bathroom of a Bojangles' over off 77. Spicy chicken and an escalated heart rate.

I pressed 5 with my knuckle and held tight to the box in my pocket. I could pop out some of them now and no one would ever know the difference. The elevator dinged and the smell of bleach hit me. I looked for the man in the waiting room but I only found a Hispanic lady and her young son asleep on her lap. She stroked his hair with one hand and clicked the remote with the other.

"You see a blond guy in khakis? Looks like Paul Newman?"

She shrugged her shoulders and went back to flipping channels. I walked all over that floor and never found him. He never came back to the shop. Now I'm walking around with speed in my purse and hell if I haven't taken it out a few times.

Though I can't seem to throw the stuff away, I tape Janine's kindergarten photo to the box. The morning the photo was taken, she wanted to wear her yellow corduroy overalls. I tried to put her in a red skirt and mock turtleneck because I thought it would look good with her chin-length hair. I promised her cupcakes if she'd just cooperate, but there she was immortalized in overalls, a gap in her baby teeth.

So many promises lay like paint over wallpaper, waiting for some change in temperature to peel. The night I left them, I waited until Hardy was asleep. I'd packed my bag three weeks earlier—the day after I met Brandon. I was just some girl in a crowd until he noticed me. At the after-party, we had one of those booze-fueled talks, out on the stoop of his apartment. It was the first hot night of the year and somehow, we got caught up in it, droplets in thick air. Brandon watched, all eyebrows and interest, as Tawni read my cards. "In essence," she said, "You need to stick to the women in your life." Either those cards were geniuses or Tawni was trying to snap me out of it. Brandon and I took it all to mean we were destined to be together. Turned out it was just sweat, booze, libido, and a similar taste in music. Damn musicians.

I'm supposed to write a letter to Janine and not send it. I have a lot of letters to write. A lot of shit to put down. She still looks at me like I'm a hunk of moldy cheese she's found in the back of the fridge. I am someone to be dealt with. I have about that much use to her. I'm grateful she has her father, but I still worry it did a number on her, not having me.

I doubt she knows, but I kissed her cheek the night I left. When I look at her, that's what I see—a girl in a Miss Piggy nightgown with a Glo Worm under her arm and her feet covered in stuffed animals. So much peace and potential.

I drive over to Janine's store and sit in the parking lot for a while, working up the nerve. The sign to my daughter's store is purple. The letters curl just the way her handwriting used to—at the T and the S in "Tweed's." The parking lot is full for late morning. It must be the pancake house that keeps it crowded.

Stalling, I smooth and tighten my ponytail. I notice the ABC store, and feel an ache as I take a swig of my coffee. It burns the roof of my mouth. Some nights I dream of making caramel and smoking cigarettes. Though I quit smoking six years ago, I still miss it, and sometimes I still taste it on my lips. Maybe that's a sign of cancer careening in my blood. At work, I can always spot the cancer complications; they're gray-skinned, even if they aren't bald. Eyes hanging like they wish they had the courage to swallow a handful of Percocet. I could see myself living off milkshakes and searching incisions for signs of infection, putting cream on my radiation burns. The yellow of them after the purple.

My heart bangs in my head.

Yes, some days I wish the world would get on with it. What

that makes me, I don't know. Maybe it's normal. I can still see Hardy with his hand all smashed up, trying to feed me noodles. Gary, just trying to reach me, get me to talk, pulling at my shoulder, touching my face. Me buried so far down in an invisible bunker I can't tell them how pointless their affection is.

I turn off the ignition. The doors swing open now and then. Maybe Janine will want to join her aunts and me at our bake-a-thon. Maybe she's a sugar-cures-the-blues kind of girl, too. When I finally go in, she's with a customer, holding a catalog and a few fabric samples, talking with ease.

"This fabric is dry clean-only but this one, this one is washable," she says, holding the blue piece up by its tiny hanger. She unclips it and puts the swatch over the back cushion of a chair next to the fabric wall. She puts the other one back.

"It would be best if I could toss the slipcovers in the washer," the woman says, rubbing her belly. I envy her nesting. Janine sees me but doesn't miss a beat. The woman leans down as best she can to pick up the fabric. "Do you have anything softer and washable? Color's good though."

"This one," Janine says, pulling out a blue stripe. "Would do well on the Newport rocker. It would hang just right. And you can wash it."

The woman spreads the two pieces out next to each other on the chair. "Can I take them home? I need to see them in her room, her light."

"Of course, I just need to get your name, number and a credit card number. They're fifteen dollars if you don't return them within a week." She folds the two fabric samples, drapes them over her arm, and looks in my direction. I don't want to bother her, so I leave her coffee with her co-worker.

"Does she like mochas?"

"Who doesn't?" he asks. "She should be done in a minute, if you want to wait."

"I can't. You have a piece of paper?"

He slides his notepad across the counter. I scribble a note

about baking with her aunts, and hope she can read my handwriting.

As I leave, the cardboard rocket ship in the window of Bedford Toys catches my eye. Maybe it will get easier with Janine. I guess things have improved with Gary. I'm unwinding my overpowering hand from his, but still staying close, trying to reconnect and find something in common. We started meeting once a week to have our own version of couples therapy out on Brenna's deck.

His car is in the drive when I get back to Brenna's. That old Jeep still ran, despite its rust spots and tacked-in headliner.

"Ready for some coffee?" I ask, leaning down to the window. He's let his blond hair get shaggy, and he hasn't shaved in a week. Patches of silver stand out high on his cheeks. We don't want anyone to know about the separation yet.

"Jesus. You scared the shit out of me."

"Sorry. Come on in."

I spoon six scoops in the filter. Brenna says my coffee's too strong, but this is how Gary and I always made it.

"We're baking tonight but I think there's a Harris Teeter pie left in the fridge," I say, leaning against the counter. "Cherry."

"I'd love some. But, I never thought I'd see you guys eating store-bought pies."

"Me neither," I say, cutting the pie, watching the cherry goo pool. "But I don't feel comfortable making a mess of Brenna's kitchen. Can you grab a couple paper plates from the microwave?"

He pulls out two each. We slide the door open, set up outside. We look out over the hill at the bare trees and eat our pie slices with our fingers, putting our feet on the railing. Sometimes we talk about our feelings. He's steeled himself against me, but I can still feel his pulse if I press hard. "You're hard to untuck."

"I know," he says. "The crust is flakier than I thought it'd be." He licks his fingers and brushes crumbs from his lap. "It's not like yours, though. I miss the chocolate. Maybe you could still make me one for my birthday."

"You can always come by tomorrow. There'll be a ton left."

"Brenna doesn't want to share with me."

"She doesn't have to know."

I think about the way Brenna's crust tastes and I can't wait for tonight. So flaky. So sweet. Store-bought crusts taste like pure vegetable shortening. All that hydrogenated fat. Brenna only uses butter.

My attention flutters from pie crust to Gary's legs. He's a runner. Always in training for some marathon. Brenna said if he'd paid as much attention to me as he did to running and his running buddies, we wouldn't be in the situation we're in. But no one outside a marriage ever really knows what's going on. There's so much ammunition in how we listen to the birds and squirrels chatter. I'm too needy to be married to a runner.

"Did someone volunteer for the Humane Society?" he asks as he looks over his mug with the picture of a spotted white pit bull.

"Yeah, Brenna did. She used to bottle feed orphaned kittens and pups. It got to be too much for her. Letting them go. Adopting them out. The ones that didn't make it. The terrible stories of where they came from. Found in an engine block, covered in grease, or wandering on their burned pads down a busy highway."

"Maybe we should've adopted a dog."

"Yeah, that's what you needed, another running partner. Besides, I don't think I could have handled it. Too much responsibility. The one that did her in was an eight-week-old Chihuahua who'd been beaten with sticks by a group of twelve-year-olds. She'd lived but had to have her jaw pinned back together. Brenna said she'd choke the shit out of the boys if she knew who they were. She coaxed and nursed her for a year until she was ready for her forever home. Tail up, eyes like a summer lake, bulging and glassy. Six months after what she thought was a solid placement, she learned that the woman who had adopted her was pregnant and had dropped her off at the pound. Brenna said when she called her, the woman didn't see the big deal. The woman seemed to have this Cinderella dream about what happens at the pound."

"I don't get it," Gary says. "What, she actually thought most of the animals at the pound were adopted?"

"Apparently. Brenna said she hated people and stopped volunteering after that."

"Sounds like it's a good thing she quit," he says, putting his coffee mug on the railing. "Guess that's why she never really tried to get to know me."

"So you're a poor defenseless animal?"

He puts his hand on my thigh.

Hardy and Brandon were much more interested in sex than Gary ever had been. Maybe it's because I was younger. Or because we were younger. Men don't talk about how their sex drives dry up. Or maybe they just get tired of fucking me. Or Gary did.

"I don't think that's a good idea," I say.

"Why not?"

"I have to meet Brenna at the store at 5:30," I say, standing up.

"It's been months, though."

"Whose fault is that?"

"Mine. Like always," he says, grinding a leaf into the deck.

"Well, it sure wasn't me that didn't want it."

"Well, isn't this you, shooting me down?" he asks, reaching for my free hand.

"We're separated. I'm not ready." I slide the door open, fold the paper plates in half, and throw them away.

"Should I still come by tomorrow?"

"If you want to." When I walk him to the door, he tilts my chin up, looks me in the eye.

"Hard to untuck yourself." He kisses me on the cheek with dry lips. I close the door behind him and watch him getting smaller through the peephole.

Gary and I both know this thing isn't working. People like Mr. Paul Newman make me feel less desperate, less muddy-headed and pathetic. Not doing things with the Mr.'s of the world is, at least, progress. Not giving into fantasies makes me less worried over feelings I still have for my first ex-husband, despite the fact that I was the one who left him, and our daughter to boot.

I fell for the wrong man in the middle of a decent marriage. Hardy hadn't handled it well, but I admired how he was with Janine. Even on the other side of Brandon, the road, and all its consequences, I can't picture myself doing the mom thing. Not completely. Full-time had been too much for me, my mental status too dependent on sleep schedules. I'm grateful Hardy lets me talk to him about Janine. What to do, how to help. He says she doesn't need help, I need to lay off. I say she does. Anyone can see the girl is depressed. If she keeps on, she's gonna wind up just like me, gay or not. I still can't quite look her in the eye. Girl sees right through me. Always did. Maybe if I bought something big from her store she'd give me a chance.

The way Janine looks at me with those coal eyes, I can see why she's good at sales. She sees right through to the simmering middle of things and pulls out just what people don't want you to see. I bet she knows when a man can't afford something but is grasping at the last shred of dignity in an overpriced "vintage" sofa. It'll dip in the middle, but Janine will make the construction shine with her story of its past. Make him feel like a man for needing it even if it was secondhand.

Those eyes of Janine's. Been giving me a once-over since she was born. The crawl of them. Back when Hardy and I were together, I couldn't take it, but now, she's just searching for answers. I'm not sure she should hear them. I'm not sure I know what to tell her. I hope, if she has a girlfriend, I'll like her.

Tonight will be good for me. Brenna usually comes home and plops down on the sofa muttering about ungrateful, entitled kids, and how no one gives a shit about learning anymore. Especially about writing and books. "They think everything I say is dumb," she'd say over a vodka and sparkling lemonade. She'd push them to notice the human condition. Yearning in Thoreau. Melancholy in *The Awakening*. Combinations of words that might set them free. O, Brenna! My Brenna! But they didn't care, she'd say. Honestly, I didn't either, but I admired her for trying. Brenna would get through one drink and then cook something spectacular. Her rhubarb pie was worth more than any of those old books. When Hardy and I were married, he and Brenna would talk about books for what felt like hours some nights out in the Adirondack chairs. I'd stretch out on a blanket with Janine, drink in hand, sometimes digging pills from my pockets, throwing them back and looking at stars until their words twirled and faded.

I wait outside for Brenna's blue teacher-mobile. In winter, everything looks clearer, tighter. Skeleton trees will always remind me of Hardy and his dad. They both used to draw winter trees, their notepads tucked in their back pockets. I think Janine did, too. Branching like rivers. Like blood vessels. Limbs. Twigs.

Between the embroidered jumpers she wears, the glasses, and the minivan, it's no wonder Brenna hasn't been on a date in two years. At least she doesn't have five layers of dog fur covering her clothes anymore. I used to think she'd be better with Hardy than I was, but he liked his girls tough. Brenna and her crate on wheels is anything but cast iron. She would joke about how supercool it was and how she was going to get me to decorate it, put some band stickers, or you know, something the kids would be into, maybe some kind of Harry Potter sticker or something. "Does Snape have a sticker?" Brenna would ask.

When Brenna walks up, I yell, "Why don't you bring your supercool cart?"

"I would, but it's full. And, bite me!"

Dorian shows up while Brenna and I look for salad. "What about asparagus?" I ask when she comes running up the aisle in her suit and heels. Though she is certainly the most polished of the three of us, she didn't inherit any of our mother's grace. She slides right into our cart, knocking Brenna from behind, and sending the lettuce in her hand tumbling.

"Dorian's here."

"Clearly," says Brenna. "Pick that up and put it back with the others."

"You're not gonna buy it?"

"No, it's all bruised now."

"What are we making?"

"Scones."

"I vote cranberry-orange," Dorian says.

"I want blueberry."

"We'll do both," Brenna says. "Will you make one of your pies?"

"Planned on it."

"Can't wait. It's good pastry weather."

We stock up on butter, sugar, heavy cream, dried berries, and chocolate-hazelnut spread. The mixed greens, oil, and vinegar look odd amid the junk. We are trying to justify ourselves. When we get back to Brenna's, we all carry a bag and unload the groceries. Brenna gets to work on the pastry dough without even needing a recipe. She has it wrapped in Saran Wrap and chilling before we can blink. She says the trick is not to over-mix or let the heat from your fingers melt the butter. Brenna gets out three glass bowls. For the scones, the three of us work on the island. Brenna and Dorian have wine. I drink diet soda and long for Vicodin. If I asked Dorian, she'd probably give me one. We whisk flour, sugar, baking soda, and salt together as instructed.

"Do you think Janine will show?"

"You invited her?" Dorian asks, looking at Brenna.

"Yes, she was brave enough to go by the store today and leave her a note," Brenna says, refilling her flour container with a new bag.

"What did she say?"

"I didn't stick around to get an answer."

"Chicken shit," Dorian says.

"Maybe she'll show," Brenna says. "I hope she doesn't have a date."

"A date?"

"I think there's a new woman. A customer. Seems professional," Brenna says, working the carton open.

I walk to the living room and peek out the window. Janine's burgundy Honda is parked across the street, speakers thumping. I wonder what she's listening to. I start to open the door and wave her in, but I think better of it. Odds are she's working up the nerve. Her window's cracked, but I don't see any smoke. She'll come when she's ready.

"Remember doing this on chairs with Mama?" Brenna asks.

Dorian says, "Yeah, she made us help all the time. I hated it back then."

"But boy did we learn how to cook," Brenna says.

"Some better than others," I say, reaching for the whisk. Brenna doesn't trust us with the wet ingredients as much. She adds the cubes of butter to each of our bowls but makes us watch her technique first.

"Blend but try not to over-handle," she says. Dorian giggles.

"Get your mind out of the gutter. How is that even dirty?" Brenna asks.

"I don't know. It made me think of fondling."

"You are twelve."

Staying quiet, I focus on "pea-sized" pieces of butter. I like the feel of the sticky flour on my fingers. We add cream and berries and form the dough into a big circle we cut like a pie. When we halve the triangles, we have three-dozen scones. It's all so zen. After we get the scones on sheet pans, Brenna turns the oven on, having waited to preheat because she didn't want the kitchen warm.

"Why don't you girls go kick back and put on some music? I'll watch the scones and finish the pie," I say, wishing for her. I follow them into the living room, lean down to look out the window with my greasy hands at my sides.

There's nothing there save for a puddle of something her car leaked under the maple tree. The streetlights flicker on.

"What about the salads?" Brenna asks.

"Yeah," Dorian says, finally flinging off her shoes, "I'm starving."

"I'll make those, too. Call you when they're ready. Dorian, you can clean when we're done."

"Fine by me."

"You sure you have this?" Brenna asks.

"Rule number one," I say. "Never walk away from the kitchen."

When they're settled in the living room, I get my purse from the barstool and pop three white pills from their foil packaging, and gulp them down with my head in the tap.

The weight of the marble roller feels good in my hands. People used to joke about me beating an ex or two (probably Brandon) with one of these suckers, but anyone who really knows me knows I would use it on myself first. I do wish the world would get on with it.

After the Fire Is Gone

The wind came up all of a sudden. I had to scramble to get the windows in the sunroom closed. It took all of my puny upper body strength to pull them down; so many years of paint coated the casings. By the time I got the last one shut, rain had sprayed my teak coffee table and floor cushions. I was ready to light candles, got out Mother's old hurricanes and everything, wondered if I should head to the liquor store but figured I'd better hunker down. Janis tapped her way over the tile, stopped, lifted a paw and gave me an eat-shit look like you wouldn't believe. "This ain't my fault, Princess Janis. Best to wipe that stink off your face." She turned, flicked her tail, and flattened herself to get under the sofa. Cats.

The sunroom still smelled of opium incense even though the rain had put it out. It sat wet and sad and drooping on the windowsill. It reminded me of my dead husband's skinny little cock. Looking out the side window, I could see the slab of driveway that he had tarred himself about two weeks before he drove our Volkswagen Rabbit down past the state line to Gaffney, where he parked under the giant sunburnt ass of a peach water tower and ran a hose from the tailpipe up into the window. Emerson died in our Rabbit in peach country.

The trees bent now, almost to the ground. I hoped the old redbud would make it. I loved the knotty trunk and random shoots that gave it a disheveled look. That redbud looked like it'd been through some shit. I walked to the kitchen window and looked down at Hardy's place. His truck was in the driveway, but the storm was hitting so hard I had trouble seeing much past what was right in front of me. Looked like one of his willow oaks might come down; if it did, that'd be it for the back of his house. I wondered if he'd even care if he lost that house. I wondered if

I cared about mine as the rain and wind shoved lawn chairs and trashcans down the street, some in circles and some rolling in straight lines like toy trucks.

The transformer across the street crackled, shot sparks, and then the house went dark. The air conditioner fizzled its last breath. It was still early, barely four o'clock but it looked more like seven or eight, the cloud cover was so thick. I opened my fridge and saw a quart of buttermilk and the foil-wrapped ham I'd baked on Sunday. I smelled honey and garlic as I kicked the door shut. Anytime the power went out and the fridge went dark, it felt like the months after Emerson's death, when I was just trying to pay for gas and the mortgage and I had to let the power bill go for a bit. Insurance don't cover suicide. My dark fridge bothered me more than anything. I tried to empty it when I got my final notice from Duke Power. I took food over to Rachel and Jack Sanders and Hardy and his daddy. I didn't even want my own food. There was corn and green beans in the freezer I'd grown and frozen myself. Between my lack of appetite and the electricity getting shut off, more food went bad after he died than I would've expected. Turns out, I didn't know how to shop or cook for one.

The coroner said Emerson died sometime after midnight. He hadn't wasted any time driving the speed limit cause he hadn't left the house until after I'd fallen asleep trying to stay up for Johnny Carson. For some reason, I imagine before the carbon monoxide had done its trick, him sitting there with his knees cramped to his chest, listening to Conway Twitty and Loretta Lynn wailing about cold ashes. Cold sheets more like it. And JJ. Poor little JJ.

When I went down to claim his body, I was surprised by Emerson's choice of clothes for his suicide. I would have painted the picture in my head, set the stage just so. Maybe even considered, or tried to, how I would lay. But Emerson, he wore cutoff jeans, neon green flip-flops and a T-shirt with what looked like a grape soda stain on the belly. I stood there over his corpse, the bag unzipped, wanting to dab club soda on the purple blotches.

Weird—the things you think when you look on a corpse. I could say I wondered why he done it, but it was something I'd feared since the day I met the man. There was some strap of black floating there in his eyes that made him impossible to reach even in the beginning. Maybe that's why when we were first together, I wanted to get him naked and see what happened. We wrestled in the backseat of his Chevy for a few months. He always had this look on his face like he wanted to fuck the death away, almost angry even, like he hated me—hated me for spreading my legs, hated me for kissing his eyes and rubbing his temples when he'd start shaking. He went as close to the edge as he could get, one time covering my mouth with his hand and then bringing it down to my neck. He squeezed but I didn't stop him. It was exciting, but I never thought it'd turn into a twenty-three-year marriage. Sometimes you find yourself in the middle of the ocean before you know it.

I never loved Emerson, but Jack Sanders was a different story. We'd loved each other since the day he and Rachel moved in next to Hardy's parents. We could barely look at each other, so we tried like hell to pretend we couldn't stand each other, for everyone's sake.

Tropical storm Carson was the first to come through in a long while, but I always welcomed storms. The opium scent made its way into the kitchen now. Breathing from my diaphragm, I thought of Jack's neck stubble that grew back by late afternoon. It took hold of me from somewhere beneath my toes, from the memory embedded in my wood floors, where we'd first torn at each other long before Emerson took matters into his own hands and Rachel's Mr. Sanders (my Jack) took ill.

The first time was a few weeks after our son, JJ, died. Here, on the floor. Emerson was at work at the mill. Rachel was giving a permanent. I tried to bake a cake for the first time. Jack found me spinning, arms out, flour bag in one hand, whisk in the other. He stopped me and we let go, collapsing into each other. We carried on for years. To my knowledge, Rachel has no idea her husband

and I were in love. She was too busy being Mrs. Sanders, the pastor's wife.

I heard what sounded like a heavy, swinging creak. By the time I flung the front door open, one of Hardy's willow oaks had fallen. I couldn't tell where it hit.

Holding the banister, I strained to see through the stinging rain. My skin chilled in the weather and before long, I was drenched to my underwear. Hardy came barreling out in his Dickies and work boots, his hairy stomach exposed. He yelled something but his words disappeared in the downpour. I waved him over. He hunched his shoulders and ran across the street to me. By the time he got to my top step, his pants were wet to the knees.

"God damned tree. I wish Mother had let Dad chop it down years ago," he said, pushing his hair back. "How are you holding up, Lucille? You need anything?"

"Nah, hon, I reckon I'm okay. You might check on Rachel though. She's never done well in bad storms. Woman's got anxiety like a Labrador."

"Will do," he said. "Mind if we go in and dry off?" he asked, slicking the water off his arms and squeezing out his pants legs. Aside from that jiggle in his belly and some gray in his hair, he looked the same as when he and JJ played together all those years ago. I'm glad he wasn't killed along with JJ. I wondered if he ever thought of my boy. I barely remember the funeral, but I know Hardy was there. Sue had dressed him in his first suit. If I hadn't been juiced up on mother's little helpers, Sherry, and grief, I might remember more. I try not to think about it. Even now that Hardy's over fifty, his girl's grown, his mama's dead, I can't stand to let myself slip into nostalgia for the sound of their voices as youngsters. I'd never heard JJ's voice change. Hardy's had turned deep, like what I imagined sand hitting rock in the Mojave for a thousand years all shrunk down and sped up into one recording would sound like, if that sort of thing was possible. Nothing ever sounded as musical as those boys playing.

Hardy and I avoided each other for a long time after JJ died. I think he blamed himself. I blamed Emerson for not keeping a closer eye on them. They knew full well they weren't to go up to June Street or anywhere near the old Whitley place. It had been vacant as long as any of us could remember. That house had been built right after the Civil War, and it looked its age. The windows had been boarded up, the porch was sinking, and the bushes were so overgrown you could barely see the bottom story. The boys had been climbing the steps to the second floor when the wood gave out. JJ shattered along with the boards; he had so many broken bones. He'd been killed instantly. Hardy had hobbled home, bruised and shaken, but mostly okay. None of us ever recovered.

"Come on, in, then." I said, opening the screen door for him. "I'll get you a towel."

When I returned to the living room, he was gone. "Where'd you get to?" I called.

"In here," Hardy said, as I heard a lighter click.

"You lighting my incense?"

"Yeah," he said. "Loretta used to burn this stuff back when we were first together. Funny how smells can make you forget the bad shit." He sat on one of the cushions and stretched his legs out under the coffee table. He wiped his arms and face with the towel, then draped it over his shoulders. "Have a seat," he said. He lit the candles. They cast a moving raft of light over the table and our faces. "What's this?" he asked, picking up my old cigar box.

"Well, it used to be Emerson's. He smoked cigars occasionally."

"Mother would have killed my Dad over cigars. She wouldn't even let him smoke cigarettes inside."

"I know," I said, leaning back on my hands and kicking off my sandals. In this light, I was less conscious of my feet but wondered how the shadows affected the valleys that had formed in my cheeks years ago. "Go on and open it if you're going to. So, did the tree hit the house?"

"No, well, it landed in the yard anyway. It knocked the gutter loose on the back."

"You're lucky," I said, cocking an eyebrow as he unlatched the lid.

"Lucille? You surprise me," he said, lifting out a rolled up plastic bag.

"There's papers in there if you want to roll a joint," I said, wiping my hands together, and leaning forward.

"When did you start this?" he smiled, pulling out a paper.

"After Emerson, this time," I said. "Let me handle that. You don't look like you have much experience."

"I was always more of a drinker or, you know, the designated driver for Loretta. Someone had to be. Someone had to look after Janine."

"Right," I said. My hands moved mechanically. I didn't need good eyes or good light to do this. It was rote. I felt for the seeds and for decent-sized buds to crumble into the paper. When I finished, it looked tighter than a factory-made cigarette.

"Where'd you learn how to do that?" Hardy asked.

"You wouldn't believe me if I told you. And besides, you might run your mouth."

"As the youngsters say, Lucille, I'm cool." He reached for the joint.

"I don't think they say that anymore, dear. How old are you? Shouldn't you know better than me? I at least watch Tarantino. I can say fuck. You can say fuck, too. We can get stoned together anytime you want. I miss having a partner."

"I, uh . . ."

"I don't mean that way. You were JJ's friend for Christ's sakes." He lit the joint, sucked too hard. A hard cough took him. When he recovered, he asked again, "When did you start this? With who?"

I took several deep drags, held the smoke, and then blew it over the top of the hurricanes so some of the smoke got trapped in the glass. It swirled. "Jack and I did it together whenever we could get time alone."

"Jack Sanders? Rachel's Jack?" he coughed some more.

"My Jack," I said. "We used to sneak out after Rachel and Emerson were asleep or when they were off running errands. Sometimes, we'd drive down to Rock Hill or Gaffney and get a motel room for the afternoon."

"Wow. The shit you don't know," he said.

"Why would you?" I asked. "I mean, us old folks did everything we could to hide what we did to each other from you kids. I like to think JJ thought his parents loved each other. But we didn't. Or hadn't, for a long time."

"Did this thing with Jack happen before JJ died?"

"Tell me, first, what did he think of me—of Emerson and me?"

"We were seven, ma'am, we didn't say much good about our parents."

"Can you think of anything?" I asked, burning the tips of my fingers. I handed the joint over for the last time, hearing the screen door slamming from the wind. I lay my head down on one of the other cushions.

"He liked your cooking," Hardy said. "Always talked sweet about your fried chicken." He spoke without letting any smoke escape as his face grew redder and, finally, exhaled. "He did not like chicken livers."

Hardy reached down and pulled me up. "Come on," he said. "Let's stop thinking about this. I don't want to waste the buzz. Where's your stereo?"

"The power's out."

"Oh, right," he laughed. "I'm fucking high."

He started to sing "Hey Jude," but changed the lyrics, "Hey Luce."

"No," I said. "Just no. I can't stand The Beatles."

"It's official then, you're off your rocker, old woman." He closed his eyes, started moving his feet a bit.

"Tell me something new, son. Wait, I have an old tape recorder and some cassettes. Emerson used to tote it around with him before we got the Volkswagen with the tape player."

"If I remember right, Emerson liked Conway Twitty."

"Yeah. That's right," I said, opening the stereo cabinet. I pulled out a few tapes and what seemed like a giant piece of equipment by today's standards.

"Does it have batteries?" Hardy asked as he looked out the window.

I slid the back off and saw two CopperTops. "We're in luck," I said, clicking play.

Our feet slid past each other in what felt like genius movements. Dancing the world's never seen. I closed my eyes and imagined Jack was still alive, feeling my hands swinging heavy and the dampness of the floor spreading to my legs—a chill was coming on.

I woke the next morning, my head on one cushion, my feet on another, and covered to my elbows with a blanket. I wondered if I'd be able to get up. With some rocking and muttering to myself and a lot of leaning on the table for support, I finally made it upright. The sun shone through the windows so bright that I could see shuffle marks across my dirty hardwoods.

I surveyed the damage outside.

Hardy was already up and carting sawed-up chunks of wood to the curb. "Let me help you," I called. "I'll pull my boots on and be right over."

Hardy waved and hollered something I couldn't understand.

In my housecoat and my purple gardening boots, I walked to the back of Hardy's place. He was walking toward the fattest part of the tree on the ground with a small, electric chainsaw.

"Careful, now. Watch that cord." His arms shook. He'd forgotten to zip his fly. As he handed me a few pieces of wood, I didn't know whether to long for Jack or JJ, but I knew I loved the smell of a split tree and wet leaves. Lord, what Rachel would think of her oldest friend.

Two Pages In

In bed, I turn my pillow longways against the wall because I never got around to buying a headboard or frame, then pull out a book about artificial intelligence or anything by Douglas Adams, but lately the words run. My eyes cross and I fall asleep two pages in. It'll take me six months to finish a book this way.

Janine says I need to put a television in here, but I like it barren. I cleared the walls of my childhood bedroom when I moved back in once Dad took sick two years ago. Clean, simple. I got rid of most of the stuff Loretta and I owned together with yard sales and truckloads of Goodwill donations. I walked away with a record player, a glider and Janine's stuff. My books. I never planned on staying. Dad's room is still set up like he left it. I'm packing up his things today. The Kidney Foundation is supposed to come get everything, even his old pickup that doesn't run anymore. The transmission's shot and I don't need it, so they can have it as far as I'm concerned. I know Janine wanted it one day, but like I say, I'm not staying and she's not ready for it. Hasn't learned to drive a stick.

I think I'll move to Myrtle Beach. Maybe I can get me a job working construction at one of those condo towers. They're developing the shit out of that place. It's not the Redneck Riviera anymore. It's gone to the golfers and the Yankees and the golfing Yankees, come down from New Jersey to build their dream homes and live where it's not cold six months of the year. Some people bitch and bitch about the migration back down South, but I think it's good for us. It gives us work. Mixes the mud.

Dad's closet is a mess. He kept everything else impeccable after Mother died, trying to maintain the feeling that she had been there and Pine-Sol-ed the shit out of the place. So chemical pine clean it stung your throat. The closet was another kind of awful.

The cabinet he'd shoved in the back has drawers that won't shut for all the junk. Underwear is in with ties, a shoeshine kit, and a dirty trowel. He'd come upstairs to change clothes after working in the garden and just leave tools lying around. Shoes are thrown in the bottom. His shirts are bunched up on the top shelf. No wonder his clothes were always so wrinkled. People overlooked it because of Mother's death. Dad was one of those men who didn't know how to do much of anything after he became a widower. He used to bug me all the time, asking me where Mom kept things, especially in the kitchen.

"Don't we have a regular can opener somewhere in this house?" he asked.

"I don't think so, Dad. I think Mother switched to the electric can opener a long time ago."

"I can't figure this durn thing out," he said, trying to open a can of Beanee Weenees. I showed him how to stick it under the little tooth and let the magnet hit the lid, but he still couldn't get the hang of it.

"I'll pick up a manual one next time I go to Wal-Mart," I had said, dumping franks and beans in a pot. "Go sit down. I'll bring you your lunch."

He swatted the air and went straight to his recliner, where he pulled the orange TV tray over his knees. It didn't take the man long to learn he didn't know his own house, let alone himself. And so, he devoted himself to what he did know—his patch of ground. He stayed outside most of the time. It's where things made sense. We couldn't be more different.

It takes me four hours to clean out his closet and another two to strip his bed and his walls of what was most familiar to him. It feels like he's dying all over again. His grassy scent lingers in the John Deere hat he left on his nightstand. But I can't stay. I won't stay. Yesterday my ex, Loretta, offered to come over and help, but I know what she was really offering so I told her I'd think about it. I figured I'd go on and do it today and get it over with. He's been dead a year. He wanted me to stay here, I know it, but this place is a sandspur between my toes. I stack the boxes like two columns on either side of the front door. I make a sign on notebook paper that reads Kidney Foundation in case they come when I'm not here. I wonder if they'll take it if I'm not here. Probably not.

I stretch my arms on the door casing, leaning into it like some sort of fat, debilitated swan. My back's stiff. My arches hurt and I've got an impacted molar. I am one big ache. Because it's been weeks since my last cut, hair falls in my eyes. I hear Janine's car. It's a turbo so you can't miss it. She drives too fast and it sounds like her front tires are chomping up asphalt. I have the urge to pretend like I'm not home, but the car's out front and she has a key anyway. What would I do? Hide under the bed like a kid? I'd just get stuck. My knees betray me when I get that low. And this shoulder hasn't been right since I helped Janine out at the store. That damn store is going to kill me. It's no different than this house. Everywhere it's them. Their shadow puppets scarring, their stories dug in, set in clay earth. Mom and Dad. Janine's just trying to hold on and I'm trying to let it all go. I can't protect her anymore. I've done all I can. She's going to lose the store, but she won't admit it. I'm sending Dad out to sea, letting these tangibles that he touched connect to the living again. I hate things going to waste. I guess Janine gets that from me.

"Daddy? You home?"

"Yeah, sugar," I yell. "Upstairs."

It is muffled from the frayed carpet, but I can still hear her stomp up the stairs. "Watch the top step. Carpet's loose."

"Finally packing it all up?" she asks.

"Yeah, I figured it was time."

"Looks like you're almost done. Weird seeing his closet empty." She plops down on the bench in front of the bed. I see Dad in the way she pulls her knee up to tie her shoe. She taps the laces when she's finished like she's soothing the bow. Just like she did when she was a proud five-year-old. She's right. The closet has little left but the timbre of my father. I see him cussing the bi-fold doors, taking them off their glide, painting them, adjusting them, babying them, and kicking them the next day. I see the pencil box he kept full of contraband in the upper right-hand corner. It's where I went to steal cigarettes when I was twelve. I knew he wouldn't bust me with Mom because he was hiding them himself. He'd try to mask the smell with Old Spice and by rubbing grass and flower petals in his hands. It never worked. He just smelled like a smoky funeral parlor.

"What brings you by, dear?"

"Just thinking about this old oil burner Maddie gave me years ago. I think I boxed it up with all those masks out in the garage. It flickers stars on the wall. The candles do so well at the store, I thought I'd see if Maddie and I could work on making something like it."

I rub my shoulder, pressing down into a big knot. "When will you have time for that?"

"I don't sleep much these days. And Maddie needs something to do with her spare time. Win-win, right?"

"I hear you," I say, taping up the last of Dad's prints. I have looked at that old German man and his pipe long enough. That god-awful pine-green hat. Those creased eyes that always made me sad.

"I thought you'd be at the cemetery today. One year and all. I have it marked on my calendar," she says, leaning against the footboard.

"I don't know why you insist on recording all the bad shit, Janine. Who wants to commemorate death like you do? I know where I was a year ago. I know where he was. I know where you weren't. I don't need you to tell me."

She kicks her purse. "Jesus with the attitude, Dad. I guess you're not handling this so well."

"I'll carry it how I carry it. I don't need you telling me when or how. Last I checked I was the parent."

"I didn't mean anything by it."

"You never do," I say, throwing a stack of jeans into the box.

"I'll be in the garage if you get over your tantrum," she says, stomping off.

I should tell her to start carting her stuff home, to move it all to her own house, but I don't have the heart. That sad calendar she keeps on her refrigerator—each month made to look like old postcards. Italia. Viva la France. Greece. Shades of colors we don't see down South. Colors so blown up with light they look whiter than white. You picture Cary Grant and some hot pants on a beach, in a café smoking, pressed up against a wall. But Janine doesn't travel. She's tied to the store. She can't see it only holds her back. Something crashes in the garage and the door opens.

"What in the hell, Janine? You tearing the place down?"

"I'm okay. Everything's cool. Don't worry about it."

"My ass."

When I take a break, I fix myself some tea and sit for a minute. Some Southerners would be ashamed to admit they use a machine to make tea, but I don't care. A fancy contraption kind of like a tall coffeepot Janine gave me a while back. I keep one pitcher of sweet, one unsweet. Not everyone likes tea-colored syrup. That shit makes my teeth feel like they've grown a winter coat. Someone else pulls in the drive, but I don't recognize the motor. I head out back, to escape and take in damp air. Dad would be proud of how bulbous his hydrangeas are these days. Looking up at the steely sky, the air sinks, pressure shifts. But still, I sit. Now is as good a time as any to fess up about smoking again. My feet will look god-awful in sandals. Hairy and pale. Wide and flat and strapped to rubber. I take a deep drag, let out breath and smoke. On my exhale, there's something callous I can almost put my fingers on. An iron sound on my lips. I pretend not to hear Janine calling me to get the door.

They come face-to-face. Loretta and Janine. They don't do that often. While I sit, I hear voices; Janine's sarcasm walks through walls. Loretta's nervous laugh does, too. She doesn't expect to find Janine here. She was coming to help me. Before long, Janine slams the garage door again.

Loretta joins me on the deck. "You got one of those for me?"

I put a second one in my mouth, suck the flame, and hand it to her.

"What's wrong?"

I tell her about packing up Dad's things despite myself. I don't want to share with this woman, but she could always draw me out. I guess that's why I loved her. She looks down from the rail where she balances, but she can't understand because she still has her dad at least. I always liked her parents when we were together, but as soon as we separated, we lost touch. They never even sent Janine birthday cards more than once or twice. You'd think, since that was their only grandchild, they would've taken more of an interest. But, hell. I can't judge.

Loretta never spent much time with them, either. She left their care up to her sister. Brenna drives up to Asheville every other weekend to check on her dad at his fancy assisted living apartment out near the Grove Park Inn. It must take the sting out of being old, having a bit of money. It won't be long before Loretta understands my losses.

"Well, if you're done packing up your dad, I should get on to work."

"Okay."

"I need to get there early. Carolyn might want to give up some of her hours. Got rent now and all, since I left Brenna's. You should swing by later."

"That right? Good for you."

"Hardy, listen. Gary isn't coming around anymore. He knows it's over. The thought of going to bed with him again, hell. That was the end of it. He moved back to Asheville."

"I don't know, Loretta. Do you really think that's a good idea?"

"I don't expect anything from you, Hardy. I was just hoping we could be friends. It's something unusual when people can peel back the plastic in front of each other. Like on the new fridge in my place. I didn't even know it was there until I nicked it. I picked at it, and it came loose. First it looked chewed up and stretched in spots, then it came off in a sheet. Maybe if we work on our friendship, Janine might start to see me like you do. To forgive. Or move on, one."

"She doesn't have good role models for moving on," I say.

"No shit, but at least we're trying."

She writes her work number on my hand. The ballpoint is sharp. There, in the way my skin welts where her numbers dig in, is the Ferris wheel at the Myrtle boardwalk that's since been torn down, my mother's veiny legs in homemade Bermuda shorts, the fear and joy in her whitened knuckles. The rise and fall of the sea. My vomit in her lap. The people stuck like pins in the asphalt below, moving as if on a Tilt-A-Whirl. Kids running ahead. Parents holding hands, eating blue snow cones. My father riding with me in the haunted house, telling me I should punch the spirits in the head if they got too close. His chuckle when the power went out and the emergency lights came on and the cheap decay of specters became visible. Faded paint on a vampire. The cracked face of a particleboard ghost. Plastic, dusty rats. A drop falls on my forehead, another on my elbow; they dot my cigarette and finally put it out.

When I flick my wet cigarette over the railing, Janine's standing at the door. I motion for her to come out and she shrugs her shoulders, throws her hands in the air. It looks like she's about to throw something at me when she does because she's holding that god-awful candleholder thing Maddie made for her. You can see where she sliced too far when cutting out the stars. Janine loved it but damn if she didn't stink up the whole house with that thing as a teenager.

Janine thinks I'm losing it. She thinks everyone around her is changing for the worse. Never saw someone who hated change as much as her. What she doesn't know yet is that's what living is— knowing we have only day, night, and memory. One year. It sits like sawdust in my belly. I'd gather all the loose sticks and light a fire, but the whole of my insides will burn right alongside them.

Janine cracks the door. "Come inside, Dad. You're soaked." After a few seconds, she closes the door. It's taken her almost thirty years to learn when I want to be left alone. She wants to talk, but I'm not up for it. I'm navigating some caves here.

Back inside, I pack my books. A suitcase full of jeans and T's. I decide to paint Dad's bedroom before I leave. He needs to be covered up for good. I'll paint it for Janine. I'll leave her the house to do with what she will. I don't want it. I can see her curling up in here, hunkering down with her grandmother's things.

At Home Depot, a young girl with a lip ring tries to tell me about the benefits of satin paint. I tell her I only use flat. I don't like that shiny shit. In old houses, it just highlights imperfections, because it reflects light rather than absorbing it like flat. I look at forty different blues before picking one I'd call blue-gray but they call "Jeffersonian." Janine likes traditional colors. A lot of grays and blues and blacks. It'll look nice against the white trim and as a bonus, Dad always hated blue. Lord knows why? I skip dinner. I just work. I work until my hands give out. I get one good coat on. After I take my mother's nail brush to the paint in my cuticles, I turn in. I get two pages read.

Loretta calls at 4:30 in the morning. I've only been asleep for a couple of hours. "Come over," she says. The quiet hum of her voice is unnerving. It pulls at the space between my shoulders.

When I get there I see, like me, she has a mattress on the floor. I think about that time at her mother's house when we screwed behind the carport. I can't help it. I could just get my feet on the fence so she could get on top.

I rub my belly and she offers me drinks. Sugar drinks. Furry teeth drinks. There's no visible alcohol in her house. She wants to talk about Janine. I want to turn out the lights, smoke, and listen to *The Dark Side of the Moon*, sleep. My body weighs more than usual at this hour. I notice the couch, tell her it looks good.

"It's the only real furniture I have," she says. "And I bought it from my baby girl."

"I bet she was excited about it."

"Who can tell with her?"

"What's the deal, Loretta?" I sit on the arm of the couch. "Why am I here? Not a single car on the road. I had to strain my eyes, looking for a hint of sunrise."

"Like I said before, we're the same."

"I get it, honey. I know what you mean, but why am I here before six in the morning?"

"I just want to fix it," she says, pulling the drawstring on her sweatpants, retying it. Her hair is in one long braid and I can see the circles under her eyes now that she's washed her makeup off. She's borderline too thin. I liked it when she had more of a butt.

"With me or Janine?"

"With Janine," she says, pacing and pulling at the end of her braid.

"Give her time. Ask about her girlfriend. Show her you don't judge."

She puts on Pink Floyd without me asking. The record has a few scratches on it, but the catches sound right with rainfall. She must still prefer records to CDs. She pulls me down on the couch by my legs. I tell her I'm here. She puts her feet up on my lap. Her toes are smooth. They'd look good in sandals, with red nails. When she's almost asleep, her breaths getting deeper, I whisper that I'm moving to the beach. She doesn't open her eyes, but she reaches for my hand.

"I thought you were here."

"I am right now."

We fall asleep. We wake up late and stiff. She fixes me pancakes and chewy bacon. When she kisses me goodbye, I hold her belt loops and feel her full lips with everything I have. I see her face at seventeen; the first time we kissed was like this, against my truck. When I think of Janine, I pull back. She wipes her mouth.

"Let me know where you wind up," she says.

"You know I will. Maybe you can come for a visit," I say, though I have no intention of seeing her like this again.

When I get home, I paint. The white is still bleeding through. I put a second coat on and wait for it to dry. My thumbs throb. I call a buddy of mine that has a condo down at the beach. He only uses it twice a year for family vacations. He tells me I can stay two weeks but it's rented come June first. Two weeks should be enough time for me to find a place to live and a job. Loretta said she knew a guy who ran a landscaping business down there, said anyone who could speak English and a little Spanish could run a crew. It's been a while but I think I could manage.

When I'm about to finish putting the third coat on, Janine walks in.

"Where have you been, Dad?"

"When did you get here?"

"I came over early this morning after I called and you didn't answer. You always answer." She eyes me. "Is there anyone in this family whose eyes aren't bloodshot?"

"Does it matter where I was? I'm fine. Everything's fine," I say.

"How can you say that? Look at yourself."

I look down at my jeans covered in paint and my ripped T-shirt, my swollen fingers. "They're painting clothes."

"I'm not talking about your clothes. The painting? The packing? What's going on?"

I drop the roller in the tray. "Sit down."

"You first."

"Why don't you go make some coffee? I'll be right behind you. Let me just get this two feet I have left and wash up."

From the window, I see a heavy cloud make its move on the sun. There is little haze; the air must be clean today because of yesterday's rain. I can see Venus. I think of moons rising on Jupiter. Characters who've resided there. A ship. Captain Kirk. His alien women. A slow dip in the atmosphere. A crash. A hair painted into the wall. The time Janine pierced her own ears with a sewing needle. I asked her if it was wise. She said she had sterilized everything. I see her ear bleeding, the strength it takes to mutilate. My mother telling me how Janine amazed her, that I shouldn't get so angry about something every girl wanted. The crunched-up remains of my mother's Oldsmobile in the junkyard. If Janine can get through the chaos of losing two mother figures and stick a needle in her own ear, she can handle her own store. I can't fix it for her. My feet turn to flapping fish on the walk down the stairs, I'm so filled with dread over her judgment. I realize the Kidney Foundation didn't come by or if they did, I was at Loretta's. The boxes remain.

"I was at your mother's," I say, before I get to the bottom of the steps. Her back is to me. She stops doing my dishes. "And you're going to have to close up shop, you know that, right? Don't you? Tell me you know that." I'm a flash flood. I happen all at once. Janine turns, throws the cereal bowl at my head. I duck. It breaks against the fireplace.

"That hardly seems necessary, Janine." The porcelain beneath the purple glaze is smooth. Picking up the mess, I put the smaller bits inside one big hunk. I sweep the flecks from the mortar. A purple shard sticks under my fingernail. When I pull it out, a line of blood fills my nail. "I'm just telling you what you need to hear. Your mother and I still have a connection that has nothing to do with you. I'm not betraying you by seeing her. I loved her once. Like you loved Celia. Like an infection." Janine sits down at the kitchen table, soap still on her hands.

"Why's she trying to get us back now?"

"She's trying to make amends, baby. You could go a little easier," I say tapping the foot lever on the trash can, dropping the bowl in.

"But …" she presses her thumbs in between her brows and eyes like she always does when she's stressed. She'll start pulling on her outer lashes next. "There's no way. There's just no way. All my life I've wondered about her—about you—about you and her and what really happened."

"I don't know that there's a concrete answer, baby," I say, pulling up a chair. "Sometimes we just need to escape our lives. Tear shit up. Become Shiva, the destroyer."

She reaches for my hand, looks down at my nail. "One sec." She dries her hands and wets a paper towel. She wipes the blood away. I am floored by how we now, in her adulthood, seem to take care of each other.

"I wonder if every kid who grows up without a parent feels this way. Everyone feels so far away," she says.

"Well, baby, I had both my parents and didn't feel like I knew them much, either. I'd never tell anyone else this, but I wished for a brother or sister. I think it's different when you have a sibling. I'm sorry you didn't get one."

"Me too," she says, blowing on my thumb.

"Speaking of far away, you ever hear that Carole King song?"

"Who's Carole King?"

"A favorite of your mama's. I think you might like her."

"Why did you say that about my store, Dad? I made enough at the sale to get by another month."

"Aren't you tired of getting by, hon?"

She goes quiet, puts her head down on her arms. I go to my old record cabinet, pull out *Tapestry*. I wipe off the dust, blow on the vinyl, and examine it for scratches. I haven't played this album for years. I used to hate Carole King for making me think of that side of Loretta. Loretta's taste in music was as varied as her hairstyles. She always surprised me that way. She listened to Carole King when she would try to write. She'd wanted to be a writer when she was younger but then she had Janine and spent all of her time mothering. I figure that was part of why she left. She just couldn't face the fact that she had given up on it without ever really trying. I skip the first song. I turn it up. Piano. Soft voice. God damned memory.

Janine sobs into her forearms. I let her finish in peace and go up to my room full of unread books. I start a new *Redwall* adventure by Brian Jacques. Fantasy, not sci-fi this time. Some people don't know the difference. I turn pages. The sound of paper gives me the faintest chill. I stay awake through the first chapter. When the album stops playing, Janine moves the needle back to the beginning.

SPITTLE

Some say regret termites through a person. External grain intact, insides barely held together. There was a time for thoughts like these. A cluster of days I thought God had gilded my status as a bestselling author in his big book of fate. But I work retail, underwhelmed by the truth in making change for Snickers bars and Coke at the hospital gift shop. Whether we're gut-punched or waylaid gently off the path to the dreams we hold doesn't matter. I wanted to be a painter, too. Splat acrylic on a canvas, swirl it with my fingertips, scratch it with nails or a chisel. Marvel at all those daddy issues smeared on canvas. Hire me a circus caller and pay him to play in some beatnik gallery filled with people who drink small batch bourbon and wear long beards and thick-framed glasses.

"Come on down," he'd yell to the gallery crawlers in the arts district. "NoDa," they call it. "Come see Loretta the amazing!" But it wouldn't look like anything much. Blobs of ochre and black. White smatters. But I can see textures and feel paint harden. The truth is, I want to tear it up and start over before I've even begun. When I write, I still can't see how the threads are supposed to merge. Painting is more like playing. As a girl, I did a series of five hundred rainbows. Couldn't get enough watercolor, like I was washed in it, skin that could blend easy, build up to something. A fridge collage of gray clouds and yellow-green grass. Hues, shades, muted and loud-talking, torn out and framed in magnets, signed and dedicated, landscape and portrait, desperate and subtle. Working on top of an old sheet, I flicked bristles with my thumbs, purple droplets flying, making rain. When Janine was young, she'd put her whole hand, her whole arm into making little Jackson Pollock thunderstorms. Paint wound up on the ceiling, the walls, everywhere. Never thought to drape the walls with sheets. Some mom. I certainly never thought of using my whole body to paint. Maybe that's the vellum between artist and mimic.

Painting is prayer, a lost call to a hopeful god.

Writing is spit. Tell me why somebody'd be compelled toward the latter. Maybe I'll get a story down about a girl who spits. Put her on paper, this girl. Girl hocks loogies like a man. Digs deep. Sucks from the nose. Produces a sound like a goose. A good old redneck girl with thick thighs and big hair who has babies too young and smokes Newports. Some say I have a poor self-image. That I regret leaving my family. That every mother feels the way I felt. Some say a lot of shit any idiot knows. Tell me it's okay to have feelings even if they're negative. Like how I let my toenails get long enough to hit the edge of my shoe so they get sore.

I doodle houses and erase them. Interested in the smudge of graphite, the feel of the fleshy bit of my hand on paper. Only fragments. Sun's hard on my eyes, insistent. It's no use.

"I see you're studying."

When I turn, a man with chin-length gray hair stands with his crotch at my eye level. "Yeah, sucks. Sunday's for beer and football."

"Football season's over," he says, sitting down at my table. He pushes his hair back behind his ears. "I'm a student, too. Up at Queens. You go there?" he asks, his cup shaking.

"Nah, I'm not a student, just doing some work on my own." His Clemson shirt and baggy jeans look like he picked them up off his floor and before that, a rack in Goodwill—not the clothes of a man who goes to an expensive, private university. He looks like he needs some kind of fix and he doesn't want to be alone. I've had slick eyes like that. We addicts go through this world marked, wearing our catastrophes in our body language, moving as if made of shale.

He rambles about a class he's taking on grant writing. Setting up non-profits. I try to follow, but hell. Staring at chalk drawings on the wall, faces blur.

"Name's Mark."

"Loretta."

He takes the lid off his cup, leans back in his chair. "I don't know, man. I just don't know. I think this teacher's got it in for me because I'm an old fart who's been through this stuff. I mean, I used to run a for-profit drug treatment center down Fayetteville. I wrote a three-hundred-page proposal. Got federal approval. These kids, they don't know. They don't understand what the world's like. They don't know how hard it is. People say, I mean people say they don't want these kinds of facilities whether it's a shelter for unwed teenage mothers or what, a rehab place. People don't want it in their neighborhoods. When it comes down to it, they're scared of falling property values and their kids being around degenerates like me."

This must be what I sounded like when I was still drinking. Wonder if Janine sees me this way, turned out and full of nonsense.

"I used to be in the music business," he says.

"I can see that. You a musician? Let me guess—a guitarist?" I spent time with my share of musicians after I left my first husband.

"Nah. Sound guy. Learned the business out in L.A. back in the '70s. Worked with The Dead some. Been in rehab with Johnny Cash."

"Johnny Cash?" Everyone tries to lay some claim on Johnny. Drifting, I'm with my ex on the shore, dragging a chair down to the water, toting a cooler full of Bud. I'm in Janine's girlhood room, looking at her collection of Mardi Gras masks, faces made of feathers and ceramic. Some glittered, some glazed, some the size of her palm. One time I'd sent her one from Vegas, but her dad sent it back to me with a note saying she'd outgrown them, that I should keep it for myself. Mark's voice has gone low, his cracked lips, conductors. Whispers about heroin. How weed should be legalized. I'm an out of whack tuner.

"Glad I never got into hard stuff. Since my cousin showed for

Christmas years ago all methed out, I swore I'd stick to booze and pills. Except coke. Coke doesn't count, right? But yeah, Melissa, she crashed under my grandma's tree. Girl looked glittered, lifeless," I say.

"And June Carter, too. Most people don't know that but I was in rehab with her, too."

To my knowledge June never went to rehab, but I nod and close my notebook.

"I learned on analog. You probably don't know what that is. You could get a four-track and make your own demo in those days."

"I know what analog is. I came up with musicians. Had an uncle that recorded bluegrass. And I took up with a rock band in the '80s, but I'm about to head out."

"I can take a hint," he says, looking into his cup with eyes like a frost-coated windshield.

"Man, it ain't you. I'm meeting my sister."

"What were you working on?"

"Just a story." I rub my fingers together to get rid of the smudge.

"Maybe you'll let me read it sometime. Maybe I'll see you again."

"Maybe. Listen, Mark. Don't give up."

In my car, I write: *Purple eyelids & old liquor.* I try to imagine the rest of his day, but I can't make it form anything. I write Janine's name at the top of the next page, start a letter, but it's just another form of spittle, gathering in the corners of my mouth. I lick them clean and drive to Brenna's house to see if she's left yet. With deep breaths from the abdomen, I put my left hand to my belly.

I'm learning to enjoy Brenna. My sister, though she's completely uptight, has this beauty in her—the way she is about food, how she is with students. I wish I could be that way about anything. It's like I go through life without. My skin moves in some mismatched rhythm with my internal organs and I can't get it synched. The clouds and grass in my paintings were never the right colors. Didn't match the image in my head. Nothing ever does.

The chatter quieted down some when I got pregnant with Janine and when she was a baby. I would sit on my knees at her crib, my hands looped through the pale yellow bars, and stare until I couldn't hold my head up anymore. Life grew. I got out of my own head for once. The day she started kindergarten I was so proud, I bent down to her, told her she could do anything, she would do anything, that she would blow those kids away with her brilliance. I noticed she'd missed a button when she dressed herself. The dress Hardy's mom had sewn for her sagged in one spot and stretched tight in another. I told her it was a magnificent mistake then fixed it for her, and for a while after that, she'd say, "Mama, I've made a magnificent mistake." She put her hands on my face, told me she'd be okay, and then skipped inside with her Strawberry Shortcake lunchbox.

I tried to keep everything tidy. We fell into a routine. I did what I was supposed to: made lunches, went to PTA meetings, cleaned her ears, helped her with her homework, baked pies, and cooked meals with vegetables. But then, the uneasiness crept back in. I gurgled and ran. I left my baby girl and her father behind. I splayed myself out on a man I thought was perfect and tried to forget all about them. But Brandon and I were a toxic mess, the same brand of crazy. We married and divorced within a year. He met some other girl and I moved around for years working shit office jobs. Sometimes I miss the mundaneness of it, the simplicity of sending faxes and filing spreadsheets, answering phones. At least it didn't stick with me like the customers at the hospital. Too many prayers and losses running loose. Makes me wonder about God when I'm supposed to yield to that higher power.

The azaleas in front of Brenna's house have already browned. Brenna comes to the door in her "I'm not a teacher today" outfit of leggings and an oversized Union Jack T-shirt. Her wet hair leaves circles on her shoulders.

"What are you doing here?"

"Nice to see you, too. Just thought I'd come by to see if you were still here. See if I could ride with you."

"I guess six of one, half dozen of the other."

I move past her into the living room and plop myself down in front of her television. Paula Deen's on. "Your favorite, y'all."

"Don't you know Southerners only eat butter and mayonnaise? Rest of the world thinks we live on fried chicken and biscuits."

"You know you love some chicken and biscuits, Brenna."

"Grrr. Yeah, well. I like Vietnamese food, too."

"Fair enough."

"Let me go brush my teeth and we'll go."

I let my shoulders down a little, unclench my jaw. Paula fries cupcakes with one of her boorish relatives. It's shameful, but my mouth waters. The cake sponges up that grease and gets brown at the edges. Drizzled with orange glaze, it looks more like Krispy Kreme by the time she's done with it as the citrus sugar slips down, pooling on the plate. Makes me want to crack it with a toothpick once the glaze sets.

It takes so much, this being present and sober. I'm exhausted, but changing the things I can as much as possible. So far, I've only done well with Brenna and Janine's dad. He's moved on. He's gotten over it. He's a good man, trying to make his way just like I am, trying to deal with what he's lost. I picture him standing knee-deep in ocean water with the memory of that Ferris wheel pumping in his veins, waiting for the big fish to grapple with his line. It brings me peace, that image.

The flyer for the new Matthews farmers' market says they're closing off part of the street just like they do at the Labor Day festival. Though I long for spring air perfumed with funnel cakes, I doubt they'll have any. It'll be hippie shit like goat cheese makers and free-range chicken farmers. I'm still not real sure that makes a difference. I mean, isn't a dead chicken still a dead chicken? Brenna says they'll probably have crafts, too. Lye soap and felted hats that women with names like Sage make with their hands. Brenna hopes they'll have tomatoes, but says it might be early yet. She knows that kind of thing. Cooks seasonally and fusses at me for buying strawberries in winter. Says the carbon footprint's massive and a lackluster taste isn't worth it. I just want strawberries when I want them; the ones shipped in from California taste all right to me.

"Let's go," Brenna says as she returns with Princess Leia knots in her hair.

"Aren't you a little old for that?"

"I'll wear my hair like I want when I'm not teaching. I don't give a damn about old. It's cuter than a ponytail and manages the frizz."

"Whatever you say." I turn my head to keep from laughing in her face. She punches me on the arm.

"Let's get out of here," she says. "I'm driving."

Her van is immaculate except for the Wendy's bag in the backseat.

"Oh, let me throw that away."

"I'm surprised you'd eat that, honestly. Let me guess, chicken sandwich, fries and a Frosty."

"I skipped the Frosty, smartass. I had papers to grade—don't judge me, Miss I-Still-Eat-SpaghettiO's even though I'm pushing fifty."

"You put enough hot sauce and cheese on them and they're pretty good. I don't guess I can smoke in here?"

"No smoking," she said and turned on NPR. "It's almost time for *All Things Considered*." I fake snore. She puts her middle finger up in my face. "It's my car."

The farmers' market isn't as crowded as I thought it'd be. Brenna says most people come early in the morning so they have the best pick of the produce. I think about the housewife up at 6 A.M. on Saturday and wonder about whether or not she's content, this faceless woman, searching for the best-looking veggies for her babes. I could've been her. I'll bet she makes the baby food herself. I hung up my apron when I found Janine preferred the jarred stuff to my mushy messes of sweet potato. Brenna should have been the one to have kids. She would have been much better at it. I tried too hard and with some things effort goes a long way, then hits a wall. I was the teenager who realized I couldn't paint anything but rainbows and gave up. Janine mimicked my perfectionistic behavior; I caught her turning all the bottles and containers in the fridge so their labels faced forward. She organized her toys and books. She straightened pillows. I made Janine worse.

She would wake in the night, screaming. No matter what I tried, I couldn't calm her. I stroked her head; I gave her warm milk, played soft music, kept the lamp on, slept on the floor next to her. Nothing worked. I couldn't fix it. It comes naturally to Brenna, though, this nurturing. Janine loves her to no end, goes to her for advice, calls up and asks for pastry recipes and I watch quietly from sofas and passenger seats this relationship I wish was mine. I guess I tried to control everything. I'm trying to be okay with the fact that all I've got right now is Brenna. I can't accept this spiritual health mumbo jumbo as part of my problem. The divine? An ever-loving hand? Gilded book of fate? I just don't see it anymore.

"Oh my God, sugar snap peas," Brenna says, running over to the next stand. "Hand me my bag," she says. "I have to buy these."

"All of them? Really?"

"I'll take what's left anyway," she says, loading up her bag, handful after handful. She pays the man wearing sandals with socks in cash. I can't imagine what she's going to do with all those peas. I know I won't eat them. Sunday supper with Janine and her girlfriend? She'll roast a chicken and steam the peas, mash some potatoes and can the rest.

We move down the lane and a woman in her early thirties stops Brenna. On her hip, she holds a dark-headed child who looks like she dressed herself. Brown cowboy boots. Green tights. A blue polka-dotted dress. "Miss Helms," she says, "Is that you? It's Sheila. I had you for advanced junior English in 1996. Fifth period."

"Why, yes, of course, Sheila. How are you? Is this beautiful little creature yours?" Everyone seems to love Brenna. She complains all the time, but after twenty years, she's one of the few that gets any kind of respect in the classroom. They talk for a few minutes while I wander away. I'm not in the mood for another introduction. I approach a cardboard box filled with a turbulent yellow sea. Chicks. Easter's already come and gone. Brenna talks with wide hand gestures. Before long, the mom hands her little girl to Brenna. Her small hands barely fit around Brenna's Princess Leia hair.

I kneel next to the chicks. They chirp. They shiver. They're terrified of all this activity. There's no mother hen. I wonder how long they need a mother. I helped my grandma raise a lot of kittens when I was young. I'd seen them born, watched their mother lick their privates to make them defecate. I have no idea what type of mothering a hen does. Is there a hen equivalent to a mama cat carrying her baby by the scruff? When I lower my hand into the box, they brush up against me. Still downy, more fur than feather. One of them pecks at my ring, thinks the sapphire is food. My grandmother had chickens on her farm. I can still see her hand down in a bucket, scattering feed, from the time they were this size until it was time to wring their necks. Sunday supper again. Crispy skin.

I buy a chick. A redheaded woman in hiking boots puts it in a small white box and pokes holes in the top with her pencil. The box looks like something you'd expect to get from the bakery, maybe filled with angel food cake. With the box in both hands, I look toward Brenna. She probably won't understand. She hands the girl back to her mother, hugs them both; with her back to me, I can see her reusable bag and its "green living" message beneath an image of Earth reaching its clownish hands out for a hug.

With a cringe, I wonder how I got here after so many nights spent backstage watching guitarists get off while they played. That's something I never knew until I dated musicians. They get hard up there. The pulse and the scream of feedback, the air sinking with stage smoke. All that sensory detail goes straight to one place. The amplifiers vibrate us all and leave us wondering what happened to our eardrums and our backs. Buses and the smell of sweaty leather. Radiating burns the day after. I crept up on myself then, came to in the backseat of a van headed to Amarillo eighteen months after leaving Hardy and Janine. Long-haired men leaned against me and a landscape whirred by that was not unlike my blurry paintings.

Hocks loogies like a man. Sweaty pits. God damned right.

"That girl was a terrible student. I don't know how she wound up in the advanced class. Couldn't write worth a damn. Did her final project on Walden with pages cut from an encyclopedia and drew a crude picture of Thoreau. At least she remembers me, I guess. She says my class was her favorite, but then, what would she say coming face-to-face with me like that? It's weird to see kids like her with offspring. I can't believe this girl who used to fall asleep in class and didn't know the difference between a semicolon and a comma is somebody's mother. I am officially old." She notices the box in my hands. "What do you have there?"

I cradle the box in my palms, looking down at Brenna's teacher hands—calluses on her writing fingers, thinning skin, brown spots I never noticed before. "I've been wondering Brenna—do you believe in God?"

"Is that God in the box?" she asks, her head tilted.

"You got me. I've bought a tiny god at the farmers' market. Seriously. That's what you ask me when I ask you that question? Sometimes, I don't know what to say to you anymore," I say, looking at the ground. "It's a chick. I thought I'd raise it for eggs. I have some room at the new place. There's a small back yard."

"Maybe I can get a few, too," she says. "We can raise them together at your place. I'd love to have fresh eggs to cook with. I haven't had any since grandma went to the nursing home. Remember how we used to sit in the coop waiting for them to lay an egg, the noise they'd make when they did, the look on their faces when we took the egg from them, that time we cracked one and it was bloody. I don't think I went back out there for a year. Grandma laughed at us, said that's how life was. Sometimes you had a pretty egg frying up in cast iron and sometimes you were scraping off the bloody mess."

"You didn't answer my question," I say, feeling the gentle scrape of the bird's feet on the bottom of the box.

"Do you?"

"I want to. I try to."

"Me, too," she says, looking off toward the horizon. "Let's buy some more chicks." She hands me her bag. I watch her crouch down in front of the box. Her leggings are so short and tight she almost tips over. She picks four. The tightness of the line in her forehead eases. On the ride home, she says, "Something told me they were the ones. They were the least active of the bunch."

If I could paint us in that moment, true and warm, maybe I could stay intact.

GIRLS LIKE THAT EAT
LEMON POUND CAKE

What irked me most about Maddie was how much she reminded me of Alexandra. She had the same fair skin and blotched, purple lips. When Alex was little, she'd burn before I could blink. Those days we didn't slather kids in Coppertone. A little color on the cheeks never hurt a child as far as I could see.

Mr. Sanders, her daddy, didn't approve of little girls running loose in the neighborhood. The time she caught her skate in a storm drain, her knees and hands bearing the brunt of it, he was so angry he couldn't even look at me. When I woke Mr. Sanders from his hard Saturday nap, he mumbled how he was starting to understand Job the redeemer. He swatted the air and went after her shirtless. When he came back with her in his arms and blood smeared across his chest, he pushed past me to the bathroom where he dropped her in the tub, skates and all, and turned the shower on. Poor Alex like a beat dog, whimpering and wet, still trying to hold her back stiff in defiance, but failing miserably. She was just a girl.

These gals next door, Maddie and Janine, though, I just don't know. They sit out in the back yard in bathing suits, drinking beer, playing hoodlum music. Maddie all done up in cherry red and a kerchief on her head. They lay on those plastic tri-fold chairs next to the garden beds, put lotion on each other's backs. Makes you sick.

I got the word. When I saw her turning up the earth for peonies, it was like those clumps of hard red clay were speaking to me. Those spindly arms of hers with tattoos down to her elbows begged for someone with a hearty dose of Luke, Matthew, and Paul.

She gets out there with short shorts on and I can just see Mr. Sanders turning over in his grave; my husband couldn't stand a tart. God love and keep his soul. He sure was a decent man—never tried much with me after my Alexandra was born. Maybe on our anniversary. I was lucky enough to have my own bedroom with a full-size bed to myself. He slept on the porch most of the year and in the front room where I did hair when it got too cold. I kept a day bed in there with daisy linens and bolster pillows for waiting clients. It wasn't much. He complained about the pillows and the industrial dryer, but when it came time to contribute to the mortgage, he didn't seem to mind my studio so much. He liked saving money on haircuts, too. I kept his clipped close. Short hair and neat nails. And call him Mr. Sanders not Jack.

"What are you at, Rachel? You look like you're going to come out of your rocker staring dimes into that girl," Lucille said.

"I'm just rocking. Don't worry about me."

"What did she do to you anyway? She's just hoeing the garden. I reckon she's keeping it up for Hardy while he's away," Lucille said as she stood to stretch and crack her neck.

"I don't guess he'll be back now that he's gone down to Myrtle Beach. He's got to get on with it," I said, unbuttoning my pants, letting my stomach breathe. "Doesn't she know what she looks like, with that trash on her arms and those shorts up her rear end? I'd have a heart attack if Alexandra did something like that to herself."

"She's got more than what's on her arms. Cardinals on her back—they're kind of pretty with that bright red."

"Maybe you think it is, but it's still a sin."

"You and your Bible talk. Keep on and I'll stop coming over. Who is she anyway?"

"Her name's Maddie. She keeps with that daughter of Hardy's. She's a lesbian, you know."

"Well, Rachel, I don't reckon that's any of our business. That's not the same girl that used to come around with Janine when she was little, is it?"

"If it is, she got uglier. Devil's done come up with the weeds.

You can't stop the dandelions. Used to drive Mr. Sanders wild."

"Mr. Sanders? Mr. Sanders? I'm so tired of hearing about the dearly departed. Jack's been dead eight years."

"He was a good one."

"A good one? I'd say that's one loon's opinion, dear. You were satisfied well enough being the preacher's wife. Where's the attention now? Where's all that Christianity? Look," she said. "There's a dandelion under your dogwood."

"Shouldn't you be getting home?"

"You're not getting rid of me that easy. We have dinner plans and I aim to keep you from doing whatever it is you have in your head to do to Janine and Maddie. Leave those girls alone."

I got quiet after that, let Lucille pick at the leaves on my clematis vine. We were like that—the two of us had been friends so long we didn't have to say much though she'd only gotten quiet after her son JJ died. We'd just chew on our lips and know what the other was thinking. She moved into the neighborhood in 1961, just like I did. Just like Hardy's mama and daddy. After JJ passed, Emerson, Lucille, William and Sue would come over every Sunday evening for supper. Little Hardy and Lucille took it the hardest. Since he'd lost his best friend, we all thought spending time with Alexandra might help. He always had a little racecar with him, even in church. He was a quiet boy, though, so it didn't bother anyone.

One evening at supper, Hardy dropped the thing and went crawling under everyone's legs, vrooming up and down our limbs. Alexandra got under there with him, took his spare Corvette. She flicked the back end, crashing it into the wall. They got along well down at our feet. It made Mr. Sanders giggle something awful and the incident flicked the fire in him that wanted a son. But he got diagnosed with diabetes shortly after our daughter was born, and they say that makes sperm bad so Mr. Sanders never fathered a boy.

I was fine with just Alexandra and didn't want to go through the mess of labor again anyway. I don't remember much, but I know it nearly killed me. They tell me I turned white and rolled off the gurney, almost bled out, but I still remember her sleepy almond eyes and knowing her name was Alexandra. We slept there, breath on breath, her tiny hot body on my chest for what seemed like days.

Part of me had hoped maybe one day Alex and Hardy would wind up together.

Alexandra was not the scholar Mr. Sanders hoped for. He wanted a boy to wrestle with in body and theology. The thing that disappointed him most was how she failed to question things. "Very few women have the intellect," he always said. He looked at her with distrust. He never believed girls could be obedient. Maybe because all those sins he listened to perpetually swarmed in his head. He took on some of the burden of them, I know. What he found troublesome is what I loved best about our daughter. That obedience and simple gaiety of hers made me know I'd have someone with me at the end, no matter what.

I suppose she proved Mr. Sanders right when she moved to Atlanta and left me here. Her timing wasn't great. She told me the same day I lost Mr. Sanders on the other side of town when he had wandered away from me in the grocery store. By the time I paid for the groceries, he was gone. We found him in the Payless two streets over trying on tennis shoes. He had quit preaching by then and had started walking to try to keep up his strength. He'd walk to the end of the street and back, taking the same route Alexandra had as a child in skates. It was when she helped me pull off his new Nikes and tuck him in that she told me.

"Darling?" he said to Alexandra. "Do you remember that time I found you dancing, covered in cake flour and we made love on the floor?"

"I would think not, Dad."

"Shame," he said, drifting off.

"What's that about?"

"I have no idea. He's out of it. What did you need to talk to me about?"

That's when she spilled it. Her husband's new job in Atlanta. They'd known awhile but didn't know how to tell me. I will never understand what hornets nest in people makes them want to run when we need them most. Anyway, Bruce isn't much of a Christian, but Alexandra is and she keeps quiet, cares for her man, takes the kids to Sunday School and fellowship on Wednesdays. She calls me when Bruce is out. When we speak, I can hear her hand over the receiver, the click of a lighter.

Kids don't turn out how you picture them.

Alexandra and Hardy were good kids. Hardy never did a thing wrong until he ran off with that drunk he met in school. I thought it would break Alexandra's heart, but she never showed it. She never asked about him or even looked his direction. That mother of Janine's had hair that must have been a good eighteen inches long. I was happy when I found out Loretta left him. I thought it was the best thing for him and Janine, but now that Janine's turned out a gay, I can't say for sure. Maybe if her mother had been around she would have turned out regular. Maybe if they'd gone to church after the divorce. Maybe if I'd prayed harder for all of us.

The door slammed shut, but I kept rocking. Lucille tired of me easily these days, said I was about as much company as a stump. A breeze came up, spun my ferns.

Maddie was still out in the yard, leaning on the hoe and pulling her bra strap up. It was coming and I didn't intend to curb myself. I tell it like it is. It's why Lucille was about the only one that could stand me and she spent half the time over here in the den watching trashy movies or cooking since I didn't do much of that anymore. I don't see much point. I can eat a can of soup without all the fuss of having to wash and chop vegetables. God doesn't care if I take advantage of Campbell's now that I don't have family. I thank Him, even for that simple ability to turn the can opener and pour. Some people can't even do that. I count my blessings.

When I was twenty and my husband's daddy got down, I testified for him. He couldn't speak since the cancer had eaten up his voice box. I laid my hands on his head, stroked the few wisps of hair back, and said, "Hush, now. Jesus is going to carry you home. All you have to do is ask." He turned his head from me at first, but I kept at it, turning to hymns. I spoke words from the classics. Words about twilight, darkness deepening, and breaking day. Everlasting light and life.

"Hope is God, you know. It's only the Almighty's voice takes up that dark veil."

His nurse said later he'd died with his finger in the hymnal, marking the page I'd read him. My father-in-law may not have been able to say it, but I know by the way he squeezed my hand that he heard. He went to Jesus. He'd been a drunk all his life. I take full responsibility for turning him at the last minute, before he hit the wall and dropped from the morphine haze into fire. I wonder if you can be a good man and a drunk. Ever since then, I try to testify when I see fit. I felt it coming with these girls. I prayed on it. Prayed over Alexandra and Hardy. Prayed over Lucille. Prayed for myself.

Inside, I found Lucille in my easy chair, smoking Mr. Sanders's pipe and watching *The Good, the Bad and the Ugly*.

"Heavens, Lucille, You couldn't be more like Mr. Sanders right now if I'd cut you from cardboard and pinned you to that recliner." Lucille bit the pipe as she leaned the chair almost horizontal. "All you're missing is a book light and a Bible."

"I'll bet Mr. Sanders never sat here thinking what I'm thinking about Clint Eastwood in those pants."

"Don't be vulgar." Though I had to admit to myself there was something in the creases around his eyes that warmed me.

"What can I say, I love a cowboy. Come on in and put your feet up, you must be exhausted from thinking about the heathens next door."

"I was praying. It's not funny. I don't want them dragging down the neighborhood. It's my duty to save them. My Christian duty. They can't see."

"My ass. Sit down. I'm going to get in there and make dinner in a minute. Just let me finish this pipe," Lucille said.

We watched television in silence, the room filling with smoke. I plotted how to help these girls. Maybe I could take them tomato seedlings. I'd spend some time with the Lord and ask for scriptures to share, that way I could mark the pages with Post-its. Maybe I could even write an outline for them. I hated to picture what went on in that house. I thought maybe I'd send a letter to Hardy, let him know what was happening next door just in case he didn't know Janine was living with another woman.

Lucille got up and banged around in the kitchen with my cast iron. She turned the flame up high for bacon. When it was done, she laid the strips out on paper towels and poured cornbread batter in the grease. It was the same way Mama would have done it. The same way I did it when Alexandra was still young. I wondered if Alexandra made cornbread for her kids. If Janine made it or Maddie, if either of them cooked. I couldn't picture them in the kitchen.

As we nibbled bacon and cornbread with honey butter for supper, I was grateful for Lucille. I missed the way Mr. Sanders crumbled the cornbread and poured milk over it, saying, "Lord have mercy, you can cook." I missed the black spots in his nails he got from working on the car or the way he sat with his glasses on his head, squinting down at the Bible, saying "uh huh" to himself and biting his pencil.

He wasn't like most preachers, had more brains than pomp. His voice built and swayed like weeping willow branches. I always begged him to get loud with it, but he wouldn't. "The Lord doesn't need raised voices," he'd say, "He can hear a whisper."

"Go get my hymnal, Lucille. I feel like singing."

"I'd sooner go home and watch *Bridget Jones's Diary*," she said, raising the chair. "I like that British fella who got caught with a prostitute a while back."

"You can watch it here. Stay."

While Blondie was drinking and cussing her way around

London and dressing up like a hooker, I cleaned the kitchen and thought about when we found out Mr. Sanders had lung cancer on top of diabetes—how hard we prayed for grace, for recovery, for hope. Alexandra and I there in his sanctuary, on our knees, holding hands, staring at the brass cross.

We lost him within a year.

Now Lucille sits where he's supposed to, laughing at the sight of Bridget's rear end falling toward a camera. I don't know why she watches such a mess.

I polished the scuffs out of my porcelain sink thinking about Alexandra somewhere in the Atlanta suburbs living the life in her 4,000-square-foot house with a three-car garage and kids in private school. When she was a baby, I used to hang her cloth diapers on a line—little rectangles marching up and down the back yard, some still stained even though I'd soaked them in bleach water. When I hung the sheets, she'd run around under them while they were still wet. "Mama," she'd yell, "this smells like some place I could get comfortable." Quirky, yes, but it seems fitting now that I know her house has heated floors. Imagine life without cold feet.

I look over at Lucille's feet, swollen and callused. "Maybe we should treat ourselves to pedicures. What do you say, gorilla foot?"

"What are you talking about? My dogs look good."

"At least you don't have a bunched-up face like that one," I said, pointing at the television.

"At least there's that. Listen, I've been thinking."

"Lord, help us."

"Shut up and listen. I want to hear your plan for talking to the girls next door. I know I can't stop you, so maybe you should let me in on your master plan."

"I was trying to come up with some excuse to go over there. I think Hardy might have shears. Or I could take them seedlings. The tomato plants are ready. Past ready. I've just been lazy about planting. Hardy plowed me a spot. I hoped he'd plant them before he left."

"You need to come up with some kind of conversation other than Jesus talk. If I was them, and you jumped straight into that, I'd slam the door in your hag face."

"Hey, my face still looks pretty good. The good Lord kept me from having jowls at least. You might want to think on what you did to deserve those flaps of yours."

"Lady, you're something else. If Jack . . . I'm sorry. I mean, if Mr. Sanders could see you now." She rubbed her jaw. "I could bake a pound cake. We could take that and lemonade. Tomorrow's supposed to be over eighty."

"What kind of pound cake do you think girls like that like?"

"Does it really matter? Chocolate. Plain. What's the difference?" Lucille said.

"I bet girls like that eat lemon pound cake. Glazed. And we should take tea instead, but that sounds good. Maybe we'll just take them half if it turns out. I'll look through scriptures tonight."

"Just don't give them any fire and brimstone. It turns people off. Even Mr. Sanders knew that."

"Maybe I should just write Hardy that letter."

"No, just be neighborly. Let's take them some cake and see what the story is."

Nothing's more satisfying than good crust on a pound cake and the one we baked the next day cracked just right. I had my Bible under my arm, Proverbs marked. When we got there, Janine came to the door. Maddie was off with her boyfriend. Turns out, she's not that way. Just Janine is. We fed her and listened to stories about the house, how there'd been termite damage—how I might want to call the bug people to get my property inspected.

"I can take a look at the perimeter to see if there's any damage to the door frames," Janine said, trying not to look at my Bible. A pair of bluebirds landed on the dogwood out front. "I've been meaning to get a house for them," she said, looking at her empty feeder. "Miss Rachel?"

"Yes?"

"Can I ask you something?"

"I suppose."

"What was my daddy like when he was young?"

Lucille spoke first. "He and my son and Rachel's girl were close."

"I didn't know you had a son, Lucille. Dad never mentioned it. He talked about Alexandra some. Said she taught him to dance."

"JJ died when they were little," I said. "Horrible accident over at the old Whitley place, but I guess they tore that down before you were born."

"I'm so sorry," she said, touching Lucille's knee.

"Your daddy always carried around Matchbox cars. Had a lunchbox full of them. He grew up to be a fine young man," I said, wishing I hadn't overdone it with my hand lotion, my fingers sticky in the heat.

"And what about my mama? Did you know her back in the day?"

When I saw a lifetime of rejection on her face, I lost my nerve for trying to save her soul.

It was in the way she held herself, her countenance. She was good. It surprised me. You could tell that she worried about her friend just as much as I worried about Alexandra. She talked about this new guy and said she wasn't sure Maddie always made the best choices; she was self-destructive. Janine felt like she had to take care of everyone. She neglected herself. I could understand that.

"We only knew your mother from the few times she came to supper with your daddy. That was before they got married, see. After that, she wouldn't come over here much. Hardy mostly visited your grandparents on his own. One time she came drunk. Spent most of the time in the bathroom. Mr. Sanders knocked at the door because we only have the one and we all had to go. When she didn't answer, he tried the knob and found her sitting on the floor, her arms over her head. I remember being furious, asking them to leave, telling Hardy I'd pray for them. He said he didn't think it'd do much good, but to have at it. You were still an infant—asleep in your bassinet in the living room with this hubbub going on, a stuffed elephant next to you. Your hair was wavy even then."

"I still have that elephant," she said, looking off toward the curve in the street, toward the entrance of the neighborhood. "You know, Maddie and I have been friends since before Mama left. That's who she is, just so there's no mistaking anything. She's staying with me so I don't have to live in this big house all by myself. I'm sort of lost since I broke up with my girlfriend and moved from my old place. Maybe it's this house. I don't know."

I crossed my legs, caught off guard by her candor and surprised that I'd had it so wrong. About that time, Lucille leaned over and shoved a piece of cake in my mouth. "Have another piece of pound cake, Rachel."

I couldn't do anything but chew and listen. "We'll have to have you two over for dinner, just like the old days," Lucille said.

I swallowed hard. "Yes. You and Maddie come on over anytime. I have some seedlings I need to bring y'all for your garden. Your daddy always grew tomatoes. I figured you'd want to set some out, too. But don't put them in with the peonies, that's where he put them last year. I'd say you're strong enough to run his plow over a spot out back, at the top of the hill."

"Here's Maddie, now."

I muttered a prayer with my mouth shut and my eyes open. Alexandra would be at the park with the kids today, out running errands, or maybe planting impatiens. She always liked white flowers because of their glow in darkness. She was still here, on this driveway, spinning around the flagpole, her hand outstretched.

When I looked up the road, all I could see was a black man on a Harley-Davidson. I didn't notice Maddie's arms wrapped around his waist until they pulled in. The glare off his bald head was something else. As he turned the bike off, the air seemed to suck up into the machine for a moment. I choked on my tea, and spit it out in my lap. I moved my hands over the wet spot.

"What's this—a tea party for Jesus freaks?" Maddie asked, looking down at the Bible beside me.

Liquor stink hit me. Lucille cackled and dropped her fork. "I like her. That's some spunk."

They sat down on the glider and introduced themselves. It seemed they'd been for a ride out to Rock Hill and back. There are a lot of bikers down there, and they don't have helmet laws. Maddie's hair was clumped. She pulled it back into a high bun, lit a cigarette, and exhaled big. "I've been wondering when you two would come over."

"Pleased to meet you. Brought you some cake. Lord knows we can't eat it all. Well, we need to get on, but don't forget I have tomato plants if you all want them."

"Thanks, we'll take you up on that," Janine said.

Maddie took her sunglasses off and wiped the makeup from the sides of her nose. Her eyes on me felt like roots shifting concrete.

"We really should be getting on." I felt a pang in my elbow and numbness in my temple. "Just bring the dishes back when you finish," I said over my shoulder.

It didn't go at all how I pictured.

When I got home, I changed into my nightshirt and spent some more time with the Lord. I sat by the window in the front room, but a glare so awful came in I had to take off my glasses. Squinting, I ran my fingers over His words. Maybe I hadn't received a word after all. I looked over at my vanity. The hair gels and permanent chemicals, the spooled cotton, the combs and scissors in a jar of blue. I took a rag and some oil to a pair of my scissors. I held them up to my hair, grabbing two fingers full, trying to hold it straight as I cut four inches off. Mr. Sanders wouldn't care for it at all.

ROSEMARIE CUTS THE WORLD

When Rosemarie pulled on her hiking boots, she wished she'd put them on the heating vent. Starting out with cold, damp toes was never a good thing, but she knew she'd feel better when she got outside. The house felt tight. Henry hovered. Even her skin had started to revolt and dry out in patches on her hips.

"Don't tell me you're starting another one today," Henry said, coming up behind her. He leaned down over the back of the couch to massage her shoulders, but she dodged him. He pulled back, shoving his hands in his pockets.

"Yeah, I am. Is that a problem for you?"

"No, it's just—I thought we might spend some time together today. Go to a movie. There's that *Anna Karenina* with Keira Knightley you wanted to see playing at the Twin. Or we could go to breakfast and maybe walk down by the river and over to the bookstore or something."

"I thought you hated Stinky Face."

"Well, I do, but I'd like to take you."

"Don't bother. I'd rather get outside. I wanted to look for this one lichen I found online yesterday."

"How many terrariums do you need, Rose? Really. I'm worried."

"Well, don't. I'm fine," she said, squeezing his shoulder. "I'll be back this afternoon. Maybe after I get cleaned up we can go to Outback. Get a steak. Have a beer."

"All right, honey."

Henry tried. Rosemarie had to give him that.

Before she headed up the mountain, she checked her notebook. She wanted to gather some hard scale liverwort, look for abandoned birds' nests, and see if she could find this rare lichen. The glass jug she'd picked up on her usual Saturday morning yard sale run would house her best terrarium yet. She didn't know much about building them, but she enjoyed the quiet detail of cutting at the world and arranging it in her own little containers.

So far, all she'd had to do was keep them damp and let them get sun. Beads formed around the glass. Moss stayed green. Sometimes, there were even minute insects hopping about in an undisturbed routine. It made her feel vast and microscopic at the same time. To date, Rosemarie had populated their house with a terrarium on nearly every surface. One on each end table. Three on the island in the kitchen. Glass containers lined the sunroom. She even put one on a plant stand in the bathroom and another on their nightstand. She'd stopped counting, but Henry told her one day last week he counted twenty-seven.

To remind herself, she read her notes aloud, "Thin. Bright red fertile clubs."

The trail looked overgrown just since last week. Wild ginger puffed up over the pink markers. By this time, she knew the trees and how to get around these hills without a clear path. As she made her way down to the creek, she walked into spider webs and stepped over snails. She crouched, looking over stumps and rotting logs.

Four hours in, she finally saw it. Even the smallest red stood out in the omnipresent green. When Rosemarie bent down to slice the basal scales loose from the log, she said, "Screw you, lichen. Even you get to be fertile." A trowel full of dirt first and in the jar it went. Wiping her face with a bandana, she plopped down on the ground, exhausted and hungry. Chinese food sounded pretty good to her. Maybe she'd put on a dress and ask Henry to take her to Jade Garden.

Funny how she started to make her own little ecosystems after the HSG test. Lying there with a towel over her abdomen, the dye went in and they took some disappointing pictures of her reproductive system. She bit her lower lip from the pain, but hardened against the news. Obstructed fallopian tubes. Misshapen uterus. The physician's assistant, with her tight, concerned lips, said,

"The dye moving through your fallopian tubes might open them up a little for the next month or so, allowing for easier conception, but you still might not be able to carry to term."

When Rosemarie told Henry, he said, "That's awful, honey, I'm sorry," and made her pancakes for supper. He wasn't the best talker when it came to the hard stuff, but she'd take a short stack over a heart-to-heart any day. She had not yet found the words for this discussion—with her husband, with her shrink, with anyone. The only person she could or would have talked about it with was her sister and she had been dead a year now.

She'd eaten a lot of pancakes in the past year.

When she got home, Henry had a football game on, and had fallen asleep with a bag of Ruffles on his lap. His belly stuck out farther than she'd ever seen it, but it's not like she was in a position to complain. She barely even put on makeup anymore and had all but stopped shaving or wearing anything one might consider traditionally feminine. When grief kept coming, pouring in like the Oregon rain until all parts of her were muddy and slick, she fell out of love with Henry. Maybe she'd snap out of it. One day, after she had exhausted all terrarium energy, she would wake up more present in this world and able to hope again. But she hadn't found the right number yet. Her hands weren't finished.

She let Henry sleep and got to work. By the time he woke and found her in the garage with Nirvana on for background music, Rosemarie no longer cared about dinner.

"How long are you going to work? Are you hungry?"

"Just give me another hour," she said without looking up. The light from the kitchen hit her bowl in a way that cast shadows over the lichen's red tips.

"Do you care what we eat?" he asked, rubbing his neck the way he did when he was done with her.

"Not really." Henry started to pull the door closed. "Wait," she said. "Do you mind leaving that open? I need the light."

"I know the feeling," he said under his breath.

An hour later, Henry came back with a tray for her. He'd made macaroni and cheese this time and even poured her a glass of wine. It would be easier if he'd just go sleep with someone else and be done with it. She gulped down the wine and stepped over the food. Before long, her back hurt too bad to lean over anymore and she sat staring at the new piece.

It wasn't right. This terrarium didn't make her feel any better. Scratching at her hips and a little buzzed, she picked the bowl up with both hands, lifted it over her chest, and smashed it on the concrete. Glass and dirt spilled from the break. The lipstick lichen sat in the middle, still upright, still red.

"What was that?" Henry yelled from the kitchen.

"My life," she said.

Spaghettification

We lie on a flattened cardboard box like cats stretching up to something unseen before we settle back into ourselves. For thirteen days, we have walked near each other, but not too near. There's something in his deep-set eyes, calling me, cooling me in the deepest heat we've felt in this Carolina pine forest in a decade. Or so Mama said when she dropped me off at "artsy fartsy" camp. "Mosquitoes are gonna drink you blue, pork chop. Bottomless hot and all this rain. They'll be biblical."

Mama had a funny way of worrying, sure, but she wasn't lying. Minus air-conditioning in our dorms, we emerge blinky-eyed and greasy from our bunks at night to flit and flirt on stoops, docks, grass patches on sandy earth. Between the lake, potted palms, and a general wet stink, death by skeeter seems logical. Still, I can't take the chance of smelling like chemicals. In my head, he will remember my long braids and shoulders exhaling flower. He won't know it's hyacinth oil I stole from the same shop Mama buys "man-catching" candles. "Make something pretty," she said, arming me with seven cans of DEET, but I left the paper bag under my bed for the duration.

Our feet, now bare, wander in grass toward each other, heel to toe, propelled like tides. John Stavros, who looks like a fifteen-year-old version of the guy from *Full House*, who hates it so much he twitches when you say so, who charcoals insect portraits and has the blackened fingertips to prove it, sits down next to us, but his gaze floats over us and to the stars. That's the thing about being crammed in with other creatives—given more than a few minutes to ourselves, we turn our watery eyes skyward, like a mob of startled meerkats. Some might call it fellowship. I call it someday.

"That's Corona Borealis," he says, prattling on to himself.

We've cranked the volume on my Walkman as high as it'll go. I want him to hear Concrete Blonde and somehow absorb all that I think and am and will be in the drumbeats and bravado of Johnette's voice. I want to tell him about missing my drunken father and being left alone more than I care to admit. The sound of the key in the lock and the hollow rooms behind it. How there are problems with the septic tank so I can't paint in our yard. The wall-to-wall carpet that stinks of old shower curtain. Microwave hot dogs for dinner. But I can only say, "Listen to this. This is the acoustic version," and will my angst into the cords, down into fibers of foam earpiece covers, into the tape rolling between us until finally, our forearms touch. We sweat against each other knowing we have to say goodbye, not caring about what we painted or produced or burned up in stagecraft. Real art comes later and after. I press stop. Stick my pinky in the plastic teeth, wind it back because my rewind button is missing. "It's yours, if you want it," I say. He hands the tape back, telling me he can't for a swarm of reasons I don't hear.

Twenty years pass, but there are moments of half slumber, breaths in between wine and awake, when I still look for him. Fleeting seconds on a kitchen timer before bread and butter and garlic, which slow like they've reached event horizon. We are spaghettified like the astrophysicists say. Pulled apart into strings. Halved. Quartered. Thinned to particles. Someday I'll get to the other side of this thing. The first. The conquering woman, pin-sharp, holding him in my palms. There will be no more nostalgia for burnt paper or parasites or bloodletting songs. I purse my lips and blow him away, back into the unkempt and undisturbed from whence he came. Those smallish, stubborn bits that want to stick, to linger in my head and heart lines, become faint smudges when I rub my hands together. Maybe he only ever existed in the fire of synapses, neuron to neuron, and we were only ever branching chemicals and electrical pulses. Bumps in the brain. Granule cells. So minuscule he never wrote of hanging by fingernails or my hair like the fray of Easter basket straw or the alternate universe where our doppelgängers live entwined and safe, young stars in close orbit.

B-Sides

The sky and the trees bellow same as anything. When I drop the needle on the record, the arm is slight enough it could dissipate like chalk dust banged loose from erasers. People can only brace themselves for so long before everything's upended. I've known my share of tough. Mama and Daddy, my grandma, and hell, even Maddie in her way, but all the effort that goes into being hard wears you down just the same. A few seconds in, the song catches. Pick it up. Move past it. Same as anything.

I wasn't supposed to touch my mother's record player when I was little. She'd tucked her albums in the bookcase like squares of gold, well protected from dust in their plastic sleeves and resting in alphabetical order. The artwork. The feel of the vinyl. The variations in sounds, some so rough-and-tumble they'd hurt my ears with their screams and guitar solos and the smashing thump of the drums. Some, like that Nina Simone record, with a sound that made my shoulders ache while I twirled on orange shag carpet. It was almost more than I could bear.

ABBA made me bouncy and when I put them on I'd practice my somersaults off the edge of the couch into a mountain of pillows. Black Sabbath made my head fuzzy. Chicago: rock with horns. The *Dirty Dancing* soundtrack was one of my favorites. I'd try to move like they did in the movie, but my hips were narrow and awkward. Some of the records were smaller with only a few songs. Forty-fives. The Temptations. But my favorite was that Nina Simone record. I would stretch my arms out into the air and above my head and I'd point my toes, trying to remember what I learned in ballet. It was all about the turnout, but I never really knew what that meant. I'd try to sing along, taking deep breaths to stretch the notes but my voice was high and thin and didn't fit Nina's frame. I sounded better with ABBA or Culture

Club or even Madonna. I didn't know anything about singing then and I don't now. I still only sing when I'm alone. Tonight was no exception. I wonder sometimes about aesthetics and taste buds and if my own voice, the voice that to me sounds so much like a fiddle that hasn't been tuned, might come across as velvet to another.

Dad says I have to call my mother. Since she's sick this might be my last chance to mend what's torn. I'm supposed to let it go—the way my mother seemed flustered and distracted even when she read to me when she still lived with us. How her voice fell flat, reflecting the cotton in her head, the bubbling, festering depression. Even Curious George droned low. I like to think I can remember when Mother took painkillers, secret flashes of a hand going to her mouth and a head flung back and the countless sips of Diet Coke. I think I even remember her eyelids wavering. But the only thing I'm sure of is that right before Mother left, she had napped a lot. Curled up with her fuzzy avocado green blanket on the sofa, she looked at the television. *All My Children*, *One Life to Live*, and *General Hospital* all in a row. She'd get up and cook when she had to, but Dad eventually started picking up takeout on his way home from work. I loved the way sweet sesame chicken stuck to my teeth in a greasy crunch. Those nights Mother barely ate, but Dad and I would sit at the kitchen table and laugh about eating like bachelors. He would share his Kung Pao shrimp, and I would offer up the smallest piece of chicken I could find. He'd never take it. We'd swap fortunes. I always wished I'd gotten my father's. His always seemed better but he'd say, "Baby, I'd give anything to have yours."

I'll call her tomorrow, after breakfast, when the wine's worn off. Tonight, it's too much. Tonight, I'll finish the bottle and listen to records in a room where so much of my life has been spent. Filled with specters of who I once was and all those that have died or left, never far below the surface. All you have to do is look at the remnants of old paint colors around the baseboards. If Maddie weren't sleeping at Martin's, she'd at least get drunk with me and try to make me laugh. We could dance stupid to the Bangles or something. The dogs aren't exactly talking back to me. Lying on the floor with records spread everywhere and a bottle of wine probably isn't the best idea I ever had. Maddie would say I'm getting all Bette Davis on her, but I figure I'm entitled to mope as I see fit. I don't know what I'm supposed to feel. My mother has been trying for almost a year now to get reacquainted with me. She's supposedly sober two years. Hell, even Dad talks to her now. I can't seem to get past the nights of wishing she would call, wondering where she was, dreaming of the last pie she'd made, its buttery feel in my mouth. I've been skeptical of everyone as long as I could remember. Maybe it was her fault. Maybe it's just my nature. I don't trust anyone other than Maddie and Dad, and now he's moved away and Maddie's in a serious relationship. On top of it all, the guilt over breaking Linda's heart is stubborn and dug in. Now it's come down to just me and wine and records in this house that passed to me.

"You have to call her, baby girl," Dad said.

"I know. Just don't rush me."

"You may not have long. It's in her lymph nodes."

"What would I say to her?"

"I don't think it's the what that matters."

Drifting off, belly down on the carpet, I wonder if she's well enough to make a pie. Sometime later, I'm shot in the neck. Outside Maddie's old apartment as we walk to her car together. Maddie's clad in black skinny jeans and a red velvet tank. A hooded man walks up, shoots Maddie in the head; I fall to the asphalt and spread my hands. My hands move to the warmth at my neck. "I don't have any money, but take my cards," I whisper. Just in case, I pray, "I do believe, Dear Lord, please. Please forgive me." I don't know why I'm always praying in my dreams.

When I wake, I'm sweat and prayer stained. The arm bounces in pops of static. After dumping the last bit of wine down the kitchen sink, I go to the porch to watch another summer storm and to let the breeze dry me out. The screen door screeches behind me and I sit down on the front steps, lie back on the porch looking up at the corroded light fixture. My grandmother used to stand on a ladder and polish that brass. Once, she did it in the middle of July. She had set up a kiddie pool out front with an umbrella and a picnic blanket for Maddie and me. Maddie's grandmother lived down the street from mine and we'd both spend time there in the summers when school was out. We met the summer after kindergarten at a neighborhood barbecue at Rachel and Jack Sanders's house. We'd rolled down their steep hill—Maddie in her starched Sunday dress and me in my denim jumper. We were the only girls our age in the neighborhood so we were a natural pair, and from what our grandmothers said, we both had a rebellious streak that was like kindling. There was a picture of that day—all the neighborhood folks sitting at a picnic table with burgers and chips, the sun bouncing off bare shoulders and knees. Women wore Bermuda shorts and men wore white T's and jeans, and the moment seemed made up, everyone's hair looked so curled and gelled, their faces softened by oak shade. I don't remember eating anything that day, but I remember Maddie and my mother's rage when she saw the grass stains on my jumper. She and Dad had argued about it in the car on the way home. Dad didn't think it was a big deal, but she muttered about how we couldn't have anything nice. Anyway, she complained about me, like she always did. I was never good enough.

Maddie and I stayed outside most summer days, playing house on the front porch or playing hide-and-seek and red light, green light. Grandma made us turkey sandwiches and chips with homemade dip. That day she'd set out the pool for us, she'd decided to polish all the brass in the house and she started with that fixture on the porch; she wore red rubber gloves up to her elbows and a kerchief over her hair. "Can't contain this mess in the humidity," she'd say, patting her head. Grandpa would laugh at her, tell her she looked like a ragamuffin and he didn't know he'd married some scarf-headed woebegone. She'd tell him to take a look in the mirror at his overalls and the dirt under his nails and then they'd talk. "I don't hear you complaining about the spit shine I put to this house," she'd say. They always did their chores with softhearted teasing. Grandpa never recovered from losing her in the car accident. The house never did look right after she died, but I've got it shining now even if I don't have anyone to share it with.

Sitting up, I dig into tender elbows. Rain's coming down so hard it bounces up onto my bare feet and runs between my toes. I've never been around anyone with cancer before. I'm not sure how to react to it or even if I want to go near my mother, despite everything. Grandpa was sick for a long time, but Dad had taken care of him. Sure, I'd go visit in the hospital, but it was a distant sort of visitation meant more as support for Dad than anything. I wasn't the one making decisions about his care or talking to doctors and nurses about his stats and DNRs and all that. That was something for older people to deal with. I took Dad cheeseburgers or Chinese since he barely ever left the hospital once they moved him to hospice, but I didn't linger near Grandpa. The way his lips caked made it difficult to even look at him. His mouth had a stiff, waxy look about it already. Grandpa didn't know anyone was even in the room anyway, and when they had to resort to keeping him restrained, I stopped going upstairs altogether. I'd just meet Dad in the smoking area downstairs.

"How's he doing?" I'd ask, lighting his cigarette.

"Same," he'd say, "Hanging on but not eating. They're asking me about putting in a feeding tube."

"What do you think you'll do?"

"I reckon I'll tell them no. I don't think he'd want to live that way. And just so you know, I certainly wouldn't. Sign the Do Not Resuscitate for me."

"Please don't talk about that, Daddy," I'd begged, flattening ash segments with my boot.

"Well, this is what happens when you don't, sweetheart. We wind up not knowing what the sick person wants. It's just guesswork and it's the living that have to hold all the guilt of it. It's enough to kick my habit into high gear. Give me another light."

I wonder if Dad will come back to visit Mom, if he can deal with seeing her sick. I remember them together when I was young. That summer of the kiddie pool, they'd left me with my grandparents to take a sort of second honeymoon up in Asheville. Dad told me they'd stayed in a log cabin and hiked and whitewater rafted with two other couples. There was a photograph of Mom standing on the riverbank in jean shorts and a yellow halter, her long hair braided and hanging down to her chest. She was tan and healthy-looking. Dad was in the raft, looking triumphant with an oar over his head. Dad said the raft had tipped later that day—Mom had fallen in and come away with purple and black from hip to shin. She'd blamed Dad for making her go, and according to him, she had downed a bottle of Jack to numb the pain. He spent that evening tending a fire outside the cabin and toasting marshmallows with one of the other couples—Rod and Ruby. He recalled they were trying to have a baby. Dad never saw them again after Mom left. He guessed Mom didn't either. "They were too good for our dysfunction," he'd said. But he still talked about that week, even now, and wondered if their family stayed together.

The next morning, I wake sure of what to do. I still feel that shot to the neck. In it is a longing for my Dad and Maddie. Fire in the flesh, fading to white. Felt like losing Maddie to Martin. Losing Grandma to a city truck. Losing Dad to the sway of Myrtle Beach. Losing Celia to the wind, her fair hair flailing. And my own chucking of Linda. It was in the slow movement of warmth from inside to my grasping hand, to the asphalt, to the drying sun. I wonder if Mom has anyone besides Aunt Brenna. She's divorced for the third time, after all. I am her only child. She probably squandered any friends she had when she was still drinking. We are both good at pushing people away, from what Dad says. And hell, if Dad could still find some shred of the pie baker in her, maybe I can too. I want to believe in what Dad believes. He says I have to forgive Mom and move on before I'll ever be content or find a healthy relationship. I have my doubts. But still, there's a pang when I think about my mom hooked up to IVs and her body weakening. Isn't she, despite everything, my creator, my blood, my beginning?

This is how it will end, I think, as I knock on the door. The geraniums on Mom's steps have wilted. Buds that have dried before they bloomed stand stiff in clusters. The crepe myrtle is in full bloom, and it burns my eyes and tickles my nose. It takes Mom a while to get to the door. I wonder if she's coming and then, finally after I fiddle with the mailbox and pick at the dead blossoms, she opens the door. I'm surprised that she looks much the same as she did when she came to the store a while back. Her eyes are darker but she doesn't look sick. When she smiles, her eyes scrunch and the lines in her cheeks become more defined. She comes outside and wraps her arms around me. She collapses into a wet sob on my shoulder and I feel like pushing her off me, but I don't. I let her cry.

"I'm so glad you're here. It's almost worth being sick for you to be standing here on my porch." She leans back, wipes her eyes.

"You shouldn't say things like that, Mom. How are you?"

She cocks her head when she hears me call her Mom. "First, let's get something cool to drink. What can I get you?"

"Coke?"

"I have Diet," she says.

"How about just ice water then?"

"Be right back. I'd invite you in but the house is a mess. I haven't felt much like cleaning since I started chemo."

"I don't care about messiness."

"That's not what your father says. No, I'd be too embarrassed to let you in here."

I wait on my sick mother to serve me a cool drink in the blistering heat of late summer. Heat waves rise from the sidewalk and everything beyond looks fuzzy from the haze. It always smells like pine needles when it's this hot. I wonder how much time my mother has left in this world. Based on what Dad says, it's months maybe unless this experimental drug they're trying slows the progression. My chest tightens as I think about IVs going into Mom's arms. I can't stand needles. Last time I got a flu shot, I passed out. I'd gone with Dad to a flu shot RV they set up in the mall parking lot last winter. I felt myself slipping from consciousness into the spinning black and brightness of a faint. Dad had seen it many times before. I passed out whenever I saw any kind of real injury or whenever I gave blood. Even the medical shows on TV make me uncomfortable. There's nothing like a rerun of *ER* or *House* to give me panic attacks and disrupt my sleep. Dad laughed at the way the nurse freaked out over my convulsions. To him, it was no big deal. He told the nurse I would be fine, just to give me a minute, and the nurse yelled at us both for not telling her what to expect. "How was I to know for sure?" I asked. "I never passed out from a shot before." We joke about how when I pass out next time Dad will just step over me and leave me there on the ground twitching.

I sip from my bendy straw. The water has a squeeze of lemon and a sprig of mint. "Fancy," I say. "But good."

"Thanks," Mom says. "I'm having a problem with citrus, so I figured I'd just give it to you. I've got several lemons in there you can take home. I have sores in my throat. One of the many joys of chemotherapy."

"So how's that going?" I ask, noticing the purple-brown spots on her arms and hands. No one ever tells you how to ask questions like this. Anything you say to someone in treatment feels wrong.

"It's really kind of boring sitting in the infusion room for hours. I get annoyed with people who want to swap cancer stories, so I just pop on my headphones and close my eyes most of the time. Sometimes I fall asleep, but I usually can't because whatever chemical they're putting in my veins burns. I get cold. They cover me with warm blankets. I like that part, that and all the junk food that's left in the kitchen for us. People love to bring donuts and cookies to cancer patients. You'd think they'd bring something healthier and sometimes you see a fruit basket, but that's rare. Though I guess I would rather have a chocolate frosted donut if I'm on my way out. The nutritionist says to eat antioxidant-rich foods and all that, but I don't think eating spinach and blueberries is going to cut it. Maybe that's a bad attitude, I don't know."

"I don't know what to say."

"You don't have to say anything, baby. Just sit with me," she said. "But the worst part is the God junk. I don't know what I'm supposed to say to people when they tell me they're praying for me. Great, thanks. Thanks for that wishful thinking you're doing for me. But they're trying to be polite and supportive, so I don't want to say I don't believe anymore, that I've put any faith I've got left in the doctors."

"I imagine that does get weird. All those serenity prayers and psalms. We were never really religious. Not like Maddie's family." I fidget with my straw and my eyes water. "Your geraniums don't look so good, Ma."

"No, I guess they don't," she said.

We sit for a while staring at the street. Neighbors drive by. The chickens out back fuss at each other before settling back down again and the trees seem to stretch in the lateness of the afternoon. I hate this time of year. I long for October or November, a time when I don't have to squint every time I forget my sunglasses because all of creation's sun-bleached, even my damn eyelids. Even my arm hair has turned blonde. I run my finger down my arm and look over at Mom, sitting with her knees up in her rocker. She looks content with her hair pulled up in a scrunchie, the freckles on her face more pronounced than the last time I saw her. She had started to look like her mother, Angela. The last time I saw her was before Mom left. Angela died when I was a teenager and all I could remember about her was that she made good peach ice cream. Dad used to talk about how beautiful she was with her auburn hair and long legs. "No one had a better-looking mother than your mother," he said. "I wish you could have known her better. She was something else. Had a walk, that woman. Your Mama's got it." And as she stands and stretches, her knees crack but she walks out to the mailbox with a gait that makes me understand at long last what Dad sees. When she isn't running from everyone and throwing a chemical veil over herself, Mom has grace. Her shorts are too short for a woman her age, but she carries it well with her bare feet and white tunic. I wipe my eyes. She sees me and I look away, toward the haze.

"We should get you a porch swing."

"Now there's a plan," she says. "Come on, doll, let's go inside— as long as you don't mind the mess."

"I'll try not to."

"That's good enough for me."

I walk in behind her and she stretches out on the sofa. I grab a pillow and sit with my back to her on the floor, propped up by the sofa. The room smells like our house did when I was a girl— of butter and stale coffee. There's a document on the coffee table about Avastin, the drug that might save her. I read the whole thing and learn about organ tears and heart attacks and all the strange side effects this drug can cause. Bone pain happens in most patients. I wonder if bone pain is like when I broke my pinky toe and it sent a wave of heat up my leg and spots to my eyes and I hit the ground like a falling limb. My blood radiates. I wonder how my mother will survive this. She's never been known for emotional strength and stability, but she has a calmer air than me up there on the couch with her toes dancing as she reads the latest issue of *Entertainment Weekly*.

"It looks like Aerosmith's going to tour again after all," she says. "I hope I'm well enough to go."

"Did you know I have your record player? You didn't take it with you when you left and Dad had it all those years and when he moved, he gave it to me. It's still in that same bookcase."

"I have one I bought awhile ago. But that one was a wedding gift from your father. It was all about the music for us. More than watching TV or going to the movies. When we were young, we went to every concert we could find the money for. Both of us were wannabe musicians, I guess. I could tell you stories," she said, putting her magazine down on the coffee table.

"Ah, the stories," I said, pulling a pillow down from the red sofa I'd slept on so many times when it was still in my store. I held the pillow in my lap—a shield against something I couldn't put my finger on. "Did you really see Kiss?"

"Where do you think I got the T-shirt?" she asked with glassy eyes. "I was convinced I was going to get on the bus with them. Your dad even waited out behind the Coliseum with me. That was back when he still got a kick out of my whims." She pulled a chenille throw off the back of the sofa and over her legs. I still felt the heat coming in through the crack under the front door. "Tell you what," she said. "I'll let you have it when I'm gone."

"Gee, thanks," I said, almost breathless. "I better let you get some rest. Do you need anything before I get going?"

"I can't ask anything more, sweetheart."

When I stood, my leg was asleep. I rubbed it, feeling the limb prickle back to life. Her eyes grew heavy. I held the doorknob, waiting, failing to push past the awkwardness of wanting to embrace her and not knowing how.

In my mind, I hug her.

ABOUT THE AUTHOR

Beth Gilstrap was born in Charlotte, North Carolina. She studied literature, journalism, and rhetoric at The University of North Carolina at Charlotte and earned an MFA in fiction from Chatham University in Pittsburgh. Her short stories and essays have appeared in a number of literary journals, including *the minnesota review*, *Quiddity*, *Ambit*, *Superstition Review*, *Sundog Lit*, *Twisted South*, and *Kudzu House Quarterly*. She is editor-in-chief at *Atticus Review*.

She has been awarded residencies at The Vermont Studio Center and The Cabin at Shotpouch Creek through Oregon State University's Spring Creek Project for ideas, nature, and the written word. She still lives in Charlotte with her husband and enough rescue pets to make life interesting. Visit at bethgilstrap.com.

Photo by Tatyana M. Semyrog

The book is set in Adobe Minion Pro. Minion is a digital typeface designed by Robert Slimbach for Adobe Systems in 1990, and Minion Pro was added to the family of typefaces in 2000. Minion was inspired by Renaissance-era type. The titles are set in Adobe's version of Garamond, styled after a type developed by punch-cutter Claude Garamont (circa 1480-1561). There are several typefaces called Garamond that vary slightly from Garamont's original design.

CPSIA information can be obtained
at www.ICGtesting.com
Printed in the USA
FFOW01n0337260215
11268FF